Anthea Church teaches English and lives in Kent

D0532398

Sleeping With Mozart

ANTHEA CHURCH

virago

VIRAGO

First published in Great Britain in 2010 by Virago Press
This paperback edition published in 2011 by Virago Press

A CIP catalogue record for this book
is available from the British Library.

ISBN: 978-1-84408-636-8

Typeset in Caslon by M Rules
Printed and bound in Great Britain by
Clays Ltd, St Ives plc

Virago Press
An imprint of
Little, Brown Book Group
100 Victoria Embankment
London EC4Y 0DY

An Hachette UK Company
www.hachette.co.uk

www.virago.co.uk

Contents

All Staff – Important Announcement

Right, Jamie. I've done it and I'm very glad indeed that I didn't have to tell you that in person or anyone else come to that, the staff for example, because if I had I would have been awfully embarrassed but as I say, I mean write, I've done it, I've been.

To Tanya Wright of Bright Lights Ltd.

This is what her advert says: 'I see everyone personally. I bring love and light into people's lives. I have attended over one hundred weddings.' I . . . I . . . I. She could do with some lessons on how to vary her sentence structure, not to mention the etiquette of putting her clients first. But it's what you said you wanted me to do: inspect a 'wider' variety of the male species before settling on you, as you were 'fifty-one, and a woman of only thirty should be very careful before attaching herself too seriously to someone so much older.'

But look, Jamie, I vet the male species daily. Every woman does. Still, if it gives you the time to see that I am really very gorgeous and just the woman for you, then short of walking the streets, this is the only way I could think of to get it over with fast before you start buying leather jackets and motorbikes (or whatever your intellectual equivalent is). I mean, it could take some years to see the wide variety you have in mind, couldn't it? Where do you suppose I might come across them? In the supermarket? Buying my books online? Dear Mr Amazon, I want more than just books. (Who runs Amazon, by the way?) Walking past the yobbo pub at the end of the road? I mean, where? And now I'm thinking: can I bear it? Can I bear to be inspected and to inspect at the same time?

Because on the very morning of my visit to Tanya Bright Lights, Our Headmistress informed us that the school is also to be inspected. Terrific to-do in the staff room. Lists to do, Hand Books to do, appraisals to do, flapping to do. And a whole year of it.

During the last inspection, my protection plan was to stay out of the room when the inspector called. I told him I was talking to the children one-to-one. A few days ago, I read the report. It said that some of the lessons were rather thin and that 'in one, the teacher left students to read to themselves quietly. Some noise ensued, however.'

So, Professor Loring, you've gone into hibernation and I'm to be exposed to some nit-picking team of experts in front of whom I shall teach badly and come across as highly strung. I'd be a lot prouder if he (she?) described me as wooden.

But now let's get to it. The visit to Tanya. The Da . . . t . . . i . . . n g A . . . g . . . e n t. There, I've written it. Dating Agent.

What a snob you are, Dorcas! Other women do it.

I'm not other women.

You are. You're just another woman. Just an ordinary run-of-the-mill female woman with a bleeding heart.

I wouldn't say that.

Well, I would. So why don't you just get on with telling about it! (Your voice, Jamie, when wearing crumpled linen jacket, waiting for me to squash my too-many clothes into my too-small bag).

Right – deep breath – I got lost, of course, driving there so was late, of course. Then crunched across her drive and parked in what I thought was a convenient spot, right outside the front door of her barn conversion, and rang the bell. As soon as I saw her, I thought: No! Just as clearly as I thought *Yes* when I saw you that second time; your sober, neat but not infertile figure arriving for dinner.

'That's a very eccentric place to park,' she snapped.

She was in a business suit, one of *those* suits, nicely dyed hair, mid-fifties. Not at all the same as the air-brushed picture in her brochure. I was wearing my jogging bottoms, you know the ones that look like a towel cut into a pair of trousers, and a wonky cream top someone once brought me from Brazil. She took one look at me and had, I would guess, almost the same thought as you must have had that day: Whoever is this person who sounded so charming on the phone? And what *is* she wearing? But, you see, I thought I'd go in my casual gear. And I also thought, as all innocents do, that she would see my eyes, my being, and know that I was worthy, special, i.e that she would inspect me astutely. But no. I realise now that the key to success is a well-cut trouser suit or a silk camisole top or a linen skirt or those sheer stockings that some women wear.

Anyway, Tanya took me into her barn, sat me down, took out a clipboard and did a little spiel, which was rehearsed and so did not require her concentration. I hate it when people talk like that. Then:

'Age?'

'Thirty-two.'

'Right, thirty-two. And your name again please.'

'Dorcas. Dorcas Trevelyan.'

You should have seen her look. Jamie, I should have known then that the whole thing was a mistake. The disgust at the mention of my name was so overt that I nearly said, or would you rather I called myself something else? Tanya perhaps? I recently read in the newspaper that men with single-syllable names do well with women, whereas women with two syllables or more than one vowel are highly sought after, so really I shouldn't have to apologise for my name, should I?

'Right. *Dorkus*. And your occupation?'

'Teacher.'

'Teacher, ri-ight. And your hobbies, *Dorkus*?'

Hobbies! What are they? I could feel the approach of that sardonic nastiness which is the flip side of misery, but I repressed it (this was going to cost five hundred pounds, after all) and said flatly, 'Yoga, swimming, reading, um, going to the theatre, um, running . . .'

'So you're an outdoor person.'

I paused. Not a bit. I like being enclosed. Put me in a wide open landscape and I feel lost.

'Yes or no?'

'Yes. Well, not totally.'

'There's only a small box on the form.'

'No, then.'

'Religion?'

'Um. Christian?'

'And what *look* of man are you after, *Dorkus*?'

'Oh, a *wide* selection will do,' I said airily.

'No, it won't. I need a specific description.'

In the end, I described you. It was all I could think of. 'Big,' I said, 'but not too big.'

'Nose, mouth, shape of face?'

'I can't divide people up into features.'

'I see. But big.'

'Yes, big.'

I smiled at the obvious allusion, but she didn't join me. Too keen to get from A to B.

'Now I must tell you that I do, if you are *serious*, have a high success rate. I have attended over one hundred weddings in seven years.'

'I know. It said in your advert.'

'Would you describe your temperament as calm, Dorkus, or would any of the following words suit you better: fiery, passionate, volatile, quiet, practical?'

'Practical doesn't really fit into that list, does it? That's not to do with temperament. It's more of a skill,' I said.

'Volatile then,' she said angrily.

'Yes. No. Well, yes, yes, I would say a mix of passionate and quiet.'

'There's only a small box. Please be specific.'

'Passionate, then.'

'Good, good. And your star sign, Dorkus?'

'Leo?'

After the word Leo, there followed a terrific crash. She rushed out of the room and returned a few minutes later, saying a pair of antlers had fallen off the landing wall. That felt very unpleasant, like someone yelling at me, No! No, don't do it.

I wanted to tell her then of my ambivalence. I wanted to tell her about you, about marriage, absolutely about marriage, but she was glued to the set questions.

'The thing is,' I said, 'I am rather bothered about, well, first meetings.'

'Everyone is. As a Leo, you'd do well with a Libra. *Dorkus*?'

'Sorry, what, sorry?'

I had been trying to remember what sign you were and whether we had been deemed compatible or not by the stars.

'I said you'll be fine with a Libra.'

'Oh good. But the thing is I don't believe in astrology but when you asked about religion, what religion, I said Christian, but that's not strictly true because I believe in reincarnation and that sort of thing, but that's not to say I have anything against Jesus, but I wouldn't want you to think I am a straightforward Christian, I'm unclear on that issue—'

'I don't need to know any of that,' she said.

But you do, you do!

Then the phone rang.

'Excuse me . . . Hello Neville, how did it go? Yes . . . yes . . . Oh well, that can happen . . . Sorry Neville, there's someone on the other line . . . A second, Simon, I'll come back to you in a momen— Yes, Neville, I'm here again . . . I would suggest another go.'

Another go at what? And there I sat, waiting for her while she juggled Neville and Simon. And she had found out next to nothing about me at all and the hour was nearly up. ('It's fifty pounds for the consultation and then another four fifty for nine meetings over *however long it takes*.' It being?)

She returned to her seat, apologised for the interruption, crossed her legs and stretched her toes in her shoes in a show-offy manner, explaining that after each meeting the two persons were to report back to her. Grim. Much better to tell the person direct. 'Many people can't do that,' she said when I asked.

It was only impatience that made me sign on the

dotted line with her heavy gold biro. I wanted to get this inspection over so that I could ring you and say, there, I've done it. I've met lots of men and you're the one I like best, Professor Loring.

'It may take time,' she remarked, looking at my jogging bottoms. 'I'm very careful about each meeting.'

I don't know what happened then, but she relaxed slightly, disappeared out of the room again while I was fiddling with my cheque book and returned in a purple towelling catsuit-type get-up – worse than my outfit by far.

'I do my aerobics now,' she explained. For the first time she looked a little vulnerable.

The temptation to ring you was overpowering, Jamie. One of those confessional calls that, with the right listener, reduces the preceding scene to its right proportions, so that one can forget it. You are so very, very good at reassurance, and in my *wide* and varied experience of people (you are all wrong about my naivety), it is not just your intelligence that makes this so, but your wisdom. As if, despite your tremendous success, you've failed so many times that you have stopped worrying about humiliation.

Do you remember when I was worried about the Great English Grid, that system initiated by the senior mistress to track and record the progress of each student in the school, involving the biggest spreadsheet known to man (women are surely too sensible to love such things)? It must be done, we were told. So I started to do it and was then told, yes, good, but it must *not* in fact be done now, it must in fact be done in the month of X. And the month of X was just when something else was meant to be being done. I brought that worry home to you like a hot potato and dropped it down the telephone line into your lovely lap. You picked it up and threw it back, until the Great English Grid became a harmless game, which did not need to be won.

Tanya Wright of Bright Lights should have been thrown straight into your lap too and then bounced up to the ceiling. But she wasn't a small woman, so you might have had a job shifting her. I am afraid you will be feeling disgusted by my decision. I certainly am.

I've just been for a run. I wish the summer trees were enough. They almost are. So fragrant, so without need. I leant against one this evening. And it was not a big one, but a slim, feminine tree. Maybe I should ring Ms Wright and tell her, no, not big after all, try slim, feminine.

How hot it is.

Geography

When people are in love they can be very unkind. As though everyone else is unfortunate. When I first knew that you loved me and I was still blind to the complications that this love would involve, I'm quite sure I became malicious in my treatment of others. Or perhaps it was just the repressed malice already there, making itself evident.

There is this woman at school who is roughly the shape of Italy, long and skinny, called Miss Shifter. She spends her holidays in inhospitable places full of geography, like the Sahara or the Atlas mountains. On the whole I avoid her, but once – when my days seemed a continuous exemption from discipline because you were there beside me – she was so rude to me and I back that she sent me a card to apologise. She had barked in the staff room that she 'not just hated' but 'detested' my teaching room. I told her that it seemed to me that she not just hated but detested everything, and it made no odds to me what she thought of my room or anything else. I related this snippet to the drama teacher (a mistake, a part of my I-am-loved-by-Professor-James-Loring cockiness) and he remarked that the only place in which Miss Shifter would be actually pleased to teach would be an operating theatre. And it is true, there have been some very cut-up children to mop up after her, from time to time.

However, now I find I rather like her. I like her rigour. It makes me feel as if she's stuck a ruler down my back so that I can walk upright in the correct direction (a superior form of yoga teacher in her own way). I've been feeling very hazy since you have gone. Like a piece of cloth that needs shaking out. I can't uncrease myself or hang straight or fold myself neatly into anything.

Miss Shifter is extremely neat. She won't be drawn on any subject that borders on the personal. And what a fine attitude towards the inspection she has: 'I shan't change. I can't change and I don't believe in change.' Dead right. Her mark book is worthy of an art gallery. So good is it, in fact, that she was asked to lead a working party on the matter, in other words to 'show us how it's done'. This was in one of the numerous meetings we have had since the beginning of this term. Seated in rows in her clean-cut teaching room whose walls are covered in work, spray-glued onto coloured card, she fished out her demonstration piece and announced, 'First of all, you need to find a nice picture related to your subject, like Shakespeare for yours, Dorcas.'

'Or dessert for her,' scribbled Pork on a Post-it note.

Pork is my friend-enemy-colleague with an inner child as difficult as a two-year-old with wind. But two-year-olds can also be fun at times and he was certainly a master at reminding one that life, one's own in particular, is not such a serious business as one (me) likes to think it is.

'Desert has only one S,' I scribbled back, kicking his huge worked-out calf under the desk.

'I mean pudding,' he whispered, pointing at her stick-thin legs. 'Might remind her to eat.'

How jovial I sound, Jamie. I'm not feeling it. I'm doing that showing-off unhappy business. It jars, I know, but I've used this trick since I was a child, to survive loss.

'After lining up the picture on to your mark book, then you go on to the sticky-backed plastic,' she continued.

'I can't do that,' I perked up.

It was Pork's turn to shove me with his equally robust arm.

'Dork and Pork!' teased the head of biology. 'Behave yourselves.'

I glared at him because I dislike being paired in any way, form or context, with Pork. Our boundaries meet awkwardly and he is always crossing mine without permission. When one stands close to Pork, his whole being impinges, and there have been times when I have stopped breathing for a minute at the feint whiff of his approach. He is not as tall as Miss Shifter but he takes up more space.

It is said that teachers together are like children. I made Pork cry once because of something I said about his teaching and he kept me awake for a whole night in a fit of anger over some unjust accusation he had made about my laziness.

'That sticky-backed plastic stuff always gets creases in it, and Shakespeare would get bent,' I moaned.

'He already was,' said Pork.

'Oh shut up,' from me, with a rudeness that dogs me when vulnerable and sad. Miss Shifter ignored us, keen as she was to get on to the origami, a complicated process of paper folding that involved dividing your mark book into terms of the school year and days of the week.

Oh Jamie, after each of these meetings I wanted so very much to ring and tell you all of this. Just as I did after meeting Tanya Wright. Why? What is it about you? It is as if you bring everything to a careful halt so that it can be properly looked at and dealt with.

I came home exhausted but with my emotions, up to now miserably focused on you, folded away as I began work on my mark book. However, I had just finished supper and was about to relax in front of some loose-minded TV when *she* rang. Tanya. So soon! I thought there would be a gap of at least a few weeks. But no.

'I have someone ready for you,' she said. 'Tall, big – you said you wanted big – dark, clean-cut, artist, tour guide. He'll ring you.'

'Can't I ring him?'

'No, the man does the phoning. That's how we organise it. I think you'll like him. I have a very good feeling about it. His name is Philip Larkin.'

'You can't be serious,' I said.

'Yes. But he's no relation to the poet.'

'Is he bald?' I asked.

She missed the connection and I spent the evening thinking about Larkin's chronic indigestion and his librarian lovers.

Dorcas Larkin.

I insisted on a Saturday. Although advised by all experienced users of this stinking method of meeting people that you should keep things brief, I still felt it deserved a weekend. Mistake. At the weekend, the entire sixth form fan out across the county and take up their posts as barmaids.

'Who's that?'

'A friend.'

'You mean your boyfriend.'

'I said a friend.'

'I bet it is your boyfriend.'

'No, it is not. It's Philip Larkin.'

'Philip Larkin!'

'Yes, the very same of "Afternoons", which you studied for GCSE, and which told you that your beauty will thicken and that by doing things like barmaiding you'll be pushed to the edge of your own life. Remember?

'But Philip Larkin's dead.'

'Not today he isn't.'

'Can we meet him?'

'No, stay well away. Stick to dishing out the drinks.'

This interrogation followed us from pub to pub and the worst thing was that I longed to hug these lovely young girls with whom conversation is such an easy pleasure, from whom no topic is barred, because getting beyond formalities with Philip Larkin was like trying to pass through a ticket barrier. Every time I felt the barrier turning – wham! – it was back against my solar plexus.

It was my fault. With an arrogance particular to the hurt person, I prefaced my chat-up comments to Larkin with, 'I love a man, who, well, who I think loves me, but the circumstances are difficult, so I, well, I wanted to distract myself. It's very hard. I don't want to do it this way. And I'm not keen on Tanya Wright. What do you think of her?'

'Tanya? She's doing a job,' he answered blandly and I felt suddenly chastened by his tact. He was a nice-looking man: good, strong dark hair, and, as Bright Lights had promised, artistic. He had brought photos of his murals to show me and they were as subtle and tasteful as one could wish for.

'I'd like one of those in my attic.'

'You're welcome. Three hundred quid a wall.'

Somehow that sealed it. We were business associates, who might, if convenient, exchange talents.

'I'm sorry. Did I seem rude hugging my pupils everywhere? It's just that I'm fond of them and it's hard to get away from them.'

'It's all right.'

It was only later that I realised that my entire dating etiquette was plain rude. To mention you immediately was tactless. Why should he even bother after that?

But if only he had been more like Miss Shifter and said, 'I hate, no, I *detest* such behaviour. It is rude and I am leaving *now*,' I should have liked him a little. But the fact was his irritation softened far too easily into indifference. He was the kind of man, I predicted, who would be uninterested in one's development, both physical and emotional.

Dorcas: I've got a hell of a period pain, Philip.

Larkin: Oh well. Par for the course.

Dorcas: I think I might become a Roman Catholic, Philip.

Larkin: No harm done.

Dorcas: Do you believe in the afterlife?

Larkin: Haven't thought about it. Is there any more bolognaise?

(Such an ugly word, bolognaise; hard to spell as well.)

'Do you like football?' I asked him, as we entered the second pub.

''Course,' he said, as if liking football were a given.

'Larkin liked football as well. I always find that surprising.'

'Did he?' he said, as if bored by any further association with the poet.

I changed the subject. 'And where do you think you might meet your eligible woman?'

'Well,' he said, becoming animated, 'I've been thinking of doing some more tour guiding.'

Oh god!

'I like travelling.'

Oh god!

'And you meet a lot of people that way. It's good fun. Parties every night.'

Oh *god*!

'Getting people from A to B, that's a laugh as well.'

A huge laugh, I thought.

'And what about your murals? Don't you want time for them?'

'Six months travel, six art.'

I told him that sounded good. Which it did, if you can organise your mind that way.

'One of my colleagues does that. Terms at school, holidays in places like the Gobi desert. She must be in love with a Mongolian, I think.'

He smiled. He smiled! But oh, what an effort to elicit anything from such smooth-faced equanimity. When we parted, I told him how sweet he was. I didn't mean it. He was not a bit sweet. He was boring. He didn't answer, by which I felt humbled again. He wasn't going to pretend. Somehow that last little exchange was more painful than the whole evening put together. It exposed my tendency to appease. And because of that, as soon as I arrived home, I came up here to write to you.

I think I perhaps *am* a Christian at heart. A Roman Catholic, even. Transubstantiation is surely nonsense, but I have a strong need to confess, not to a shape behind a curtain but to someone who will genuinely bring light, shed light, lighten the burden of guilt that I so often feel because of my nature. I also felt sad that evening because I realised that to the general population, I am peculiar. I hate football, I hate travelling, don't much like parties and am incapable of getting anyone from A to any letter you care to mention in the alphabet. I predict Philip Larkin will find his woman within the next three months and that she will be blonde and good at white-water rafting. I can tell he is a 'let's forget it and move on' type of person, whereas I am a harking back type; back and back. And always to you.

Do you remember the week when you were in Cologne? We had already met, you had emailed and said that we might talk on the phone when you were away and gave the phone number of your hotel. After the brief first call, we spoke every morning for an hour before I went to school and you went off to lecture. I wonder how it was that, although you were working so hard and attending god knows how many dinners and meetings, you sounded so like a man on his bed at home, speaking peacefully and with so much laughter? Had it been me abroad on a lecture tour, I should have closeted myself in silence before and after each formality. But you, as much as you like silence, *you* talked like a river, as young and fresh and fluent. Also funny.

Perhaps it was because you were away from home and so had the child's illusion of being unobserved and free. I think that perhaps your travels have always been a respite from the intensity of being married to Victoria. Is that right?

In any case, the child-state you were in brought out an equivalent mischief in me of the kind that, reported to anyone else, would sound disgracefully embarrassing.

'What is a clitoris?' I asked on the second morning, angling for one of your lectures.

'*What?*'

'What is it?'

'You know quite well what it is.'

'Yes of course, but I want you to explain.'

'Don't be absurd.'

'Seriously, Jamie, I want you to describe it. I want to hear it from you and I want to know its exact location.'

You laughed and then did indeed assume that formal, lecturing tone that means one is in for a rest, as it will go on for some time. I lay back against my pillows.

'The site of the aforementioned is in the bottom right hand corner of America. It is like Florida.'

'But Florida hangs down. I thought the clitoris stuck out. How can something that hangs down stick out?'

'Ah, so you *do* know where it is and *exactly* what it looks like.'

'I wouldn't say *exactly*.'

'I'd like to marry you,' I said on another morning, when the subconscious had somehow catapulted me into the future and I was, while still talking like a child, a settled woman wishing for children. I meant it with all my heart, and, hearing my heart, you wept. I was so surprised. I had not realised there was so much pent-up sadness inside you. You had told me you were happy and now you were crying. I sailed on, unable to hold or explore your tears, which meant – what? You did not love your wife but had to pretend you did? You did love her but had to pretend to me that you didn't? Perhaps I didn't want to know and that's why I went on, 'I'd like to marry you *on a boat*. No dresses and guests or any of that. On a boat.'

Why a boat, I wonder? Perhaps boats indicate travelling of a kind that I like, taking one into uncharted places and yet with someone else at the helm. I think now that the combination of being both led and constantly in a state of exploration is at the crux of my requirements in love. How compliant and tender you were. Something inside you rose to meet me, recognised that I was not just playing. I loved you. I loved you at this beginning, I loved you all the way through Cologne. I still love you. And I want to travel with you. Not to Paris or Rome or any of those places but to our Selves. Self is a place. It has a capital and deserves a capital letter.

*

So let's get the meeting of our two selves quite straight. We met in a bookshop. Correct? We had coffee together. I visited your flat. You visited my house. So what, to most people. And yet, very early on, somewhere in the midst of those early meetings, I came to know that we were on a long journey together.

My other loves have been episodes, emotional day trips, which of course at the time felt more important, for someone of my nature needs to regard anything embarked upon as the chief business of life. But with us, I have a much clearer sense of the actual steps we took. For example, of that first visit after Germany, there remains in my mind the snapshot of you at the station. You standing, waiting. So still. So composed while I swerved and jiggled my way into a space and got hooted at. On the way back from the station, the station where I have picked up ten, fifteen people before and driven them gently home, asking how they are, silently slipping the gears from one to two to three, I nearly got lost.

'Sorry, this is really wrong,' I said. 'We'll end up at Sainsbury's if we go up this road. Do you want anything at Sainsbury's? Marmalade or anything? I haven't any marmalade.'

I had already sensed that although you were a liberal, an artist, an intellectual, you were a person who liked marmalade and a spoon to dish it out with. You smiled and, like a teacher – not in the manner of Our Headmistress, but gently, as if with a class of thick boys (or girls, come to that) who can't tell the difference between they're, there

21

and their – you said, 'I don't think I need anything, no. I think we should just get home. Don't you?'

Then I got completely lost. And again, you smiled and reassured, 'I should just turn round and go back, start again. Don't you think?'

And we were on our way.

You didn't think we were on our way anywhere much. You thought we were just going to go to bed and be friends. I knew otherwise, only because I had not the imagination for another option. Even at the age of thirty, my sexual experience was relatively limited. I wasn't going to be one of a list of women for any man. Unless I mattered to them as a spirit, a mind, a being, they could take a jump, and I had learnt to detect the level of their seriousness by the way they sat and spoke and looked and 'arranged things'.

Finally on the road home, I started to crunch the gears. They didn't even need changing as it was a dual carriageway, but there I was, on the flat, frantically going from second to third, fourth, fifth. Quietly, you put your hand on my neck. Ow. Remembering that hurts. As if you were holding my head on to my neck; no movement but for a slight stroke with your index finger; a lazy, pro- tective stroke. If I had stalled, you would have saved me from whiplash or else have strangled me. Those two options in balance attracted me. Philip of the murals and tour guiding, in contrast, seemed unable to hold any- thing tight. So loose was he that, had he not been called Larkin, I would have forgotten his name by now.

At last we arrived home. How I love home. Everything comes right at home. The calmness returns, the feeling of being able to compose oneself in safety. Like a lawyer, you put your small black case down neatly beside you, took off your linen jacket as if settling down to a task and we kissed. What else could we do since I had asked you to marry me on a boat? Preliminary conversation would have seemed a waste of our preciously short time.

You have no idea how strange that kiss was to me. And the way you held me. Yes, on reflection, principally the way you held me. For our kissing in itself has been a long journey, wouldn't you agree? But that first kiss felt as if a small landmass that had been split off from the mainland was being reconnected. I was your missing nose, for instance, or the lobe of your ear, whereas you were the bulk of my Self returned.

You told me afterwards, but I have absolutely no memory of it, that after that kiss, I took your bag upstairs and unpacked it, as if in expectation of a souvenir from a foreign land.

'You stupid, *stupid* girl,' Miss Shifter yelled. 'How can Rome be the capital of Paris? Rome and Paris are both capitals in themselves. You really are the *pits*.' And then she blushed, as one does when spotted indulging a bad habit. I was watching her, lover of the dessert/desert, teach a geography lesson. I wrote a note on the clipboard that had been issued to me by the senior mistress.

('As practice for the inspection, we shall be doing a series of observations of each others' lessons,' Our Headmistress had announced at one of the many weekly briefings, during which she removed and replaced her glasses no fewer than six times within the space of three minutes. 'Informal feedback only please,' she had bossed, in that voice which means the SMT – Senior Management Team – had decided upon this in one of their six-hour meetings which operate loosely around the topic of the colour of students' tights. 'And in order to give all this a lighthearted touch' – those gold shoes really do betray the soignée prankishness in her – 'we'll all pick from a hat who we are to watch.' And who did I get to inspect but Miss Shifter.)

During the lesson, a little girl with pre-orthodontist buck teeth:

'Miss Shifter?'

'What?'

'Do you know what happened when I went up the Eiffel Tower?'

'I don't see how I could know that.'

'Do you want to though? It'th quite funny.' The little girl bounced up and down in her seat.

'Geography is not *meant* to be funny.'

'Oh go on, Miss Shifter,' the others wheedled.

She glanced at me, who was smiling broadly. Oh go on, anything to get off the subject of population figures in capital cities, I was morse-coding her.

'Very well.'

'Well, I wath up the Eiffel Tower with Mummy and Daddy and Janie. And Daddy wath thaying that'th that and that'th the other, you know, thtuff in Paris.'

'Don't say *stuff*.'

'Things.'

'Sights.'

'Thights. And I said to Daddy, but where'th the Eiffel Tower? And he thed, we're on it, you fool.'

'Yes, very funny. Thank you. But now, we were talking about the desert.'

Afterwards, she sat in the staff room in a state of high tension, long legs double-crossed. It touched me that she seemed to care about what I had thought of her lesson.

'Well?' she asked, pursing her mouth, for which read: If anyone criticises me, I'll call in the union.

'You were excellent,' I said, wanting to get home.

Her mouth. Despite what I had claimed to Ms Bright Lights, I realise I can, after all, single out a feature if it is especially attractive. Miss Shifter, despite her bony torso, has a wide, almost luscious mouth.

Your mouth, Jamie. I can single out your mouth too. Of *course* yours. Don't be upset if I say that the best part of your mouth is the inside, as if your lips are turned inside out. Isn't it odd how two such contradictory features can fit together so well? You have quite an ill-defined chin, an oak-sized neck and a willow-tree mouth.

I do not know how you can push me away after I have come to know your mouth so well. Our most recent kisses were like the kisses between two women. Not hungry, devouring kisses, but varied and gentle, our heads at so many angles to each other that each time the shape of your lips felt different. But always so soft. That last day, before I left your flat, I could have sat astride you for hours, my legs bent, feet in the palms of your hands, hands on your face, angling and angling you until there was only the sensation of two mouths and the sound of my coming.

And now of your going. I do understand, Jamie. In theory I understand, but I'm trying with all my might to understand the *heart* of your departure. Or was it your head that ruled? If you ever reply, answer me that.

'He said you were boring,' Tanya Wright revealed three days after my meeting with Philip Larkin.

'Me boring? But *he* was boring.'

'I am frank with my clients. It is usually best.'

'Oh well, I do bore myself quite often,' I gave in.

'Well try not to. It rubs off.'

I started my wretched giggling again.

'So, Dorcas, it might be some time before I ring you. Oh, excuse me a moment—' (I guessed the Neville-back-to-you-in-a-moment routine was about to start up.) When she returned: 'As I say, Dorcas, it may be some time before I contact you. One can never tell what's round the corner.'

'Until you're over the hill,' I mumbled.

'Well, life is full of ups and downs.'

And there are swings and roundabouts too, I suppose, I was going to say. At that moment, I detested her. The way she used my name all the time made her all seductive charmer who is, simultaneously, ruthlessly set on business and getting to the point of a signature, 'Here if you will, please . . . and here, thank you'. I almost told her to watch herself and stay on the straight and narrow, but recognised that further rudeness would be tantamount to wasting the money I had paid her and she might dish me up a real geek if I wasn't careful. Anyway, I wanted to get back to the Great St Edmund's English Grid. Even that, which is very boring indeed, is easier than hearing it said that I myself am very, very boring.

History

Mr Eighteenth Century was the next offering from my man agent.

'I've had a spate,' she said, and again I began to feel anxious that I was being dished up the leftovers. 'As usual, he will ring you.'

A week passed and no call. How anxious I was when *you* pulled in the reins after your visit to me that first time. We had made love so immediately, so without hesitation, and a part of me had expected the pace to increase further. But you paused without explaining, something you would never do now. I wondered if you were afraid or puzzled. I wanted to ask you, to say why, what, when again? But another part of me was relieved. There is a circumspect element to my personality just as there is to yours. (Indeed, it seems to me now that you are almost exclusively circumspect, often horrified by some of your more sudden emotions.) So, as it turned out, if you had continued to rush things, left us no time to think, I might have doubted that I would ever again be able to think in peace, to sit quietly with myself and feel the quality and state of my own mind. I would have worried that my whole life would be taken up with excitement and adrenaline and phone calls and emergency passions, a momentum I would have enjoyed, but which would have been injurious to my nature.

Perhaps you had divined this danger from the way in which we had made love; not fast and impulsively, though the journey from sitting room to bed was as quick as a child's sprint to a corner shop for fags or sweets. But once there: slow and exploratory. I learnt that you liked a gradual quality of touch, the thorough feeling of a woman's body before you entered her. I loved that about you and also respected it. I told you so and you said nothing, only slowed down even more, me exploring your elbows, your neck, the marks on your back, the thickness of your arms which I love so dearly. But then, ironically, after you had gone, my child-self wanted the rush again, the rash promises, the excitement of commitment without its actuality.

But love makes one careless. I knew it too and perhaps it is that which has always made me suspicious of intimacy. One must carry one's own cross, not try to give it to someone else. I was aware, and am still, that it is only human to want to hand over one's burdens: Here, you carry my cross while I cavort about. And so the seduced lover obeys, until one day he gets fed up and drops both crosses on your foot, his and yours.

Each Monday that term, I attended a yoga class, which somehow pointed up this conflict between excitement and circumspection. One Monday, we had talked on the phone during the day and worked ourselves up over one of those stupid worldly systems that you are so wonderfully adept at satirising – recorded messages that require one to press six numbers before a human being emerges on the line, something of that sort – and I was still laughing inside as I entered the yoga room.

The teacher was a pleasant woman, but she irritated me with her leniency. I wanted her to work us hard but instead she kept insisting that we should only 'take it as far as is comfortable'. I have never favoured this approach to life but it is one that I can fall into easily. I always left her class feeling I could have done another two hours, but I had paid my money and so was going to stick the term out if only for the benefit of slightly improved posture. Perhaps she had become aware of my feelings, because she would often walk past my mat and look at me as if life and I would come to blows.

'Now,' she said, in a motherly voice. 'We'll move on to the shoulder stand. So ladies, palms flat and slow and slow and up, up with those legs, and up and up, that's it, slowly, yes.'

I became drunk with a mischief that I had taken in during a day at school with children and with you on the telephone. I started to wave my legs around. I wanted to kick her, to do a back flip and arrive nubile and irresistible in a spotlight, to a round of applause. At the same time, I felt guilty. Again, as so often with my relatively innocent gestures of defiance, I chastised myself: does love make one so terribly narcissistic? I could feel the other women with their psoriasis and cellulite joining in their dislike for this restless me who thought herself so firmly above the ordinary cruelties of deterioration.

I told you about it, about my battle between bubbly joy and grown-up precision.

'Dorcas,' you said, 'carefulness is terribly important.'

And I saw that you meant it when I encountered the interior of your study two weeks after your visit to my house. I write 'encountered' deliberately, because that room has a personality, a presence. On your desk, piled in order of size and weight, were three books you thought I should read, a folder which held six pages you had printed out, on pleasantly glossy A4 paper, of an article to refresh my teaching of *Othello*. Beside the folder was a paperweight, under which was a slim pad, on which was written half of the first sentence of a lecture to be given in six months: 'Reading is a religion to which . . .'

It was, *is* a lovely room. Entirely organised and yet so rounded and warm in its atmosphere that I felt I could concentrate in it perfectly. You had struggled to write both lectures and plays in that room, totted up the hours once, I don't remember how many but it was a great number, many of which had been difficult. But whatever had troubled you had been transmuted into a gentleness that in turn filled me with a peace that does not prohibit joy. You *are* that room, Jamie. You and you alone. It felt as if Victoria had never stepped foot in it.

On that visit, when Victoria was staying in her studio flat after a late night at work, you said to me, 'The end result of most human endeavours is failure. You have to understand that first and be calm about it. If you have to wait until you die to get recognised for whatever you have done, hard cheese.' And then the doorbell rang and a man arrived with the Chinese takeaway we had ordered, and I have never seen a pair of eyes bulge with such delight as yours suddenly did. You ripped off the lids to examine the dishes, which were predominantly pink and sloshing in sauce. I saw then that you were a person who must have his immediate sensual needs fulfilled in order to deal sensibly with this tedious delay of the deeper rewards of life.

'But why bother then?' I whined, regarding posthumous achievement.

'Oh forget that now, just enjoy the prawns.'

Outside, London stretched across the window in a flat pattern of misted lights. I thought how lovely it would be to get up each morning and drink coffee beside that window in silence. And how that would be enough. And I remember wondering too what Victoria looked like in the silk dressing gown that hung on the back of the bedroom door. It was white, good quality, elegant. Stab of jealousy. I only wear cotton.

*

'Is that Dorcas?'

'It is.'

'Hello. This is Neville.' (Oh no, not *the Neville*!) 'I'm from the Bright Lights organisation, set-up, what have you.'

'Oh, right.'

I instantly became cavalier and perhaps off-puttingly confident as I slammed the iron with which I had been struggling (clothes left too long, too dry, too creased) face down in its wire cradle. *Neville* sounded as if he had a clothes peg on his nose. I wanted to refuse all advances there and then. The voice told all. I pictured his house: chintzy, dark, secondhand furniture, eiderdowns. But I have never been good at rejecting, perhaps because I so badly dread rejection myself.

'Right then,' he said, bracing himself. 'Shall we meet?'

'All right,' I replied, dreading the loss of a Saturday of solitude, the long, lazy evening which can be late because Sunday is free of the strangulating weekday routine that chokes teachers and students alike.

'What about next Saturday?'

'Fine. Where?'

'Don't mind.'

'Right! OK. Well, I'll just get the map.'

Oh god, more geography!

'Now,' he pronounced, 'if you're coming from East Grinstead – that's where you are, isn't it? – you go straight up the A22 due north.'

'North?'

'Towards Godstone.'

This is a man, I judged, who does *enormous* spread-sheets of his personal finances and buys drip-dry shirts from Matalan. How nasty this process of arranged dating makes one, as if the safest way to manage it without humiliation is to be a bitch. But I am not a bitch, and so listening to myself poke fun always leads to a wasted hour of self-flagellation.

'To sum up,' he said, 'we'll meet by Churchill's foot at Westerham, ten o'clock, next Saturday. You can't miss the statue. It's enormous.'

'Good,' I said, meaning bad. Very, very bad.

I would have quite liked a date with Churchill. His voice was without nasal problems and he would have bawled Do it! in an open-nostriled way. I do not dislike a man who issues orders.

Which is why I so adore the way you speak. That quiet way, that slow way, then a lecture which indicates that you consider it a waste of your precious time to wait for other people's views and might just as well deal with the few important topics in life yourself. In case you need reminding, your serious topics are:

1. Books and reading books
2. Books and writing books
3. Tax and why we should pay it
4. Books
5. Sex and religion ('inseparable in my view')

6. The obscenity of drunken brawls
7. Books

Some of your less serious topics are:

1. The charms of female tennis players
2. The horror of staying in other people's houses
3. Why men should not wear shorts
4. Old people and why they should be killed off if they wish
5. Young people and why they should not wear scant clothing if they do not wish to be raped

Another familiar topic, which usually turns into a lecture I never tire of hearing, is the one about your afore-mentioned study. 'I do not like leaving my room. It is unnecessary to leave my room. My room has all that I desire from life within it. It has my books, it has the telephone, it has the computer. It has a pleasant temperature. Into my room I can bring whatever food I wish, such as sweet and sour prawns in that crimson sauce about which you were so rude. I can also see the city beside me and I can listen to music. I can think. I can write. I can read. I do not require anything else. The end.'

'Not love? Not people? Not buying a new shirt? Not landing in a new country and smelling the heat as you step off the aeroplane?'

'Dorcas. There are two types of people. There are the human doings and the human beings. Neither is worse than the other. But I am a human being. What are you?'

I struggled. I was standing once more in that place where I had felt every desire would be fulfilled simply by drinking coffee beside the window. I was unable to answer, which is not like me, and I knew then that I needed more than human being. My history told me that. I love solitude because it is a rest from company. I love company because it is a rest from myself. Together, company and solitude are my two feet. I have no wish to limp through life.

'Both, I think. I like both. Company is important but I soon want to get away from it. Actually, I don't know.'

Perhaps because of your certainty, I became able suddenly to see myself more clearly. That is: I am a little like a soldier who wants, if only out of duty, to fight, but is exceptionally pleased to get home. I have always loved going home. I could see that you were the same. The only difference was that you weren't ashamed of it, whereas somewhere inside, in my Protestant upbringing, I thought human *being* was sinful.

It is ironically because of this self business that so many hours of my life have been spent in *necessary* talking. Even the smallest of worldly battles has sometimes required two hours of debriefing. I have shouted at a class, for example. I tell Lucy, my closest colleague and friend. And as I speak it out, I feel as if I am falling into a dark, soft place where misery is the norm. Professional though she is at school, there is no morality attached to conversations with Lucy. She can take the most absurd suggestions seriously, knowing there to be a clue in them somewhere. Together, we are even capable of translating the urge to murder into the need for a meal with a touch of chilli in it.

And you, my darling Jamie, when you are listening, what is it that you do? You understand my mood without echoing it back or trawling through it: 'I should just take it a step at a time. Work for an hour. Do your teaching. Watch some television. And then start again tomorrow. Don't you think?' I love that 'don't you think?'. The reluctance to impose anything more than a tender suggestion.

There have been other times when your voice has been so distant that I have wept afterwards, the worst being when you were having lunch with Victoria and you announced in a panic when I rang, 'No, we don't want new windows just now, thank you. Goodbye.'

How that hurt me. And yet how well I understood that, caught between Victoria and me, you could say nothing other than the ridiculous.

It would have been simple had you not loved her; had you been separated or of that liberal make of person who can accommodate casual affairs into your marriage. But you did love her.

Remember how you explained one night when neither of us could sleep? How you had loved her intelligence, had chased her like a madman from the moment you saw her at university. She was the 'love of your life'.

You had noticed attractive women, of course, during your marriage, but they had never had her intelligence. They always lacked something. And it gave you pleasure each time you felt tempted, to recognise the superiority of your original choice.

I said nothing. I tried to move myself inside the warm protection of my own body. I tried to listen from the comfort of my own self-sufficiency, tried desperately not to trespass. It was hard, but I knew that your uncensored explanation was an act of generosity, a necessary warning that one day I too would be unfavourably compared. I remember telling myself, stay with your Self. Never lose your Self, Dorcas.

You turned to me then and touched my breast. 'There is one thing, though,' you said. 'There is one thing that I have found in you which I think I have sought since I was a child and never found until now.'

'Yes?' (Little voice.)

'Benevolence. Is that the word? Forgiveness. A re-entry to Eden. There is something about you, Dorcas, of that. Victoria is hard. Extremely critical.'

'Oh.'

And then you apologised for 'going on about Victoria' and I stopped you. Put my hand over yours and kept it on my breast.

Churchill's foot was magnificent. I arrived early so that I could sit on it and lean back against his massive shin, turning round once to look up at his nostrils, which were filled with stone. 'You wanted big,' Tanya had said of Philip Larkin, 'well, he's big, dark, artist, tour guide.' I realised while I was sitting against Churchill that she had completely omitted to give me a physical description of my next beau, although later I discovered that she had shown him a passport photograph of me. What cheek! (Once he had got into his stride and we had taken tea in a marquee set up for a flower show that we came across by accident on our ramble, Neville scoffed, 'You looked a bit like a horse in the photo. You're better in the flesh.')

He was late. And he had a little rucksack in which he had packed wodges of cling-filmed fruit cake and sandwiches. Not a big man, a slight man with a pleasant face, *but* feet that stuck out at right angles. I mean it. Really, those feet which tell you immediately that were he to kiss you, he would try to swallow your entire face.

'I had to queue at the petrol station.'

Oh, dull. Oh, queues. ('I never queue. I don't believe in queues. Go away and come back.' Another of your favourite topics.)

I wish there was some typography to catch Neville's wildly silly voice. Think Kenneth Williams just after an operation for haemorrhoids and you'll have it.

'Well, what would you like to do?' he asked, putting down his stupid little bag and revealing a nasty patch of peeling skin on his inner arm, which, while we discussed the options of (a) a walk and then (b) a picnic and (c) some tea, he kept scratching. We made our decision as above, and then he said, 'But we could do it all the other way round: (a) some tea, (b) a picnic and (c) a walk.' Oh god! He would take a year to choose a shirt, I just knew it, and he would definitely frequent Oxfam as an even more economical alternative to Matalan.

How telling small comments are. I turned longingly to huge, generous Churchill and wished he could rise from his plinth and take me by the hand for a stroll and a magnificently sparse conversation. I remembered hearing extracts from his letters to his wife, Clementine. They were so passionate and yet restrained in that way that men from the past knew to be sufficient. Our twenty-first-century history will be a tawdry one in comparison: all extravagance and overuse of endearments. As for you, Jamie, such was the misery I felt, that any thought of you had completely disappeared. I think I hide from you when I am ashamed or unhappy. I have not yet come to trust romantic love enough to be sure that it does not hurt a person when they are fragile.

The Happy Families atmosphere continued at St Edmund's. At the prospect of an external enemy – the inspectors – the staff had all but dropped their knickers. I'm teaching First World War poetry this term, and, as you know, Jamie, though I am knowledgeable about the First World War poets, I am shamefully ignorant of how WWI segued into WWII. For me, mud and trenches spread across the entire first half of the twentieth century. When I am asked, I just say: It happened in a trench. However, owing to the inspection, I thought I'd better get Nina, the head of history, to do a quick whizz through fifty years of battle. She agreed, but said she'd have to bring her baby in as it was her day off, and would I hold it.

'Yes, of course.'

'Which poets are you studying? Which war years? Countries? Exam course? Any trouble-makers in the group?'

All this she whispered at me at breaktime between instructions from Our Headmistress regarding the misuse of school bicycles, 'which are not, I repeat *not* to be left lying on flower beds'. As if the staff rode them round the campus during break for a laugh.

Nina's speed put me to shame. No notes, just over-heads (I liked the fact that she had never bothered to learn how to use a Smartboard) manipulated by elegant hands tipped by coral nails, while she gabbled things from memory.

I can safely say, however, that I remember now not a single fact she imparted about Germany, Allies, guns, men, rations, trenches, France, *anything*. I could only remember you. You in France on another of your lecture tours, writing to me of your distress.

We had by then sketched out a rough pattern of our loving. Dates, times of meeting, moments of battle, of love-making, though none of this had quite established itself into a shared history, or something we could draw on in any reliable manner.

And also, of course, there was your marriage. Your commitment to Victoria. I look back with regret on our early conversations about her. I have not been married. I do not understand the way in which two people slowly blend and move together so that parts of them become inseparable; not until now, now that you have gone and I see, like a disease, but a good, beautiful, transforming dis-ease, how far you have inhabited and changed me. But snatches of the battle you were fighting come back to me.

Your worry that Victoria would find out. Your worry that Victoria did not in any case love you, but was nevertheless very proprietorial. 'She might even have had affairs,' you said once in a wrenched voice, 'but to be told of me having one would cause a row I would lose, Dorcas. She is sharp, extremely sharp, and could do a great deal of damage.'

'Why bother with me then?' I had asked forlornly. Or me with you, I might have added. Or even you with her, come to that.

'Because I love you.'

'Already?'

'In the bookshop.'

And then that letter from France, which perhaps was the most revealing of all.

My darling Dorcas,
I am all jammed up. I am not a bit happy here in
France. Surrounded by these young actors who are

rehearsing my play, I feel very aware of my age. And also yours of course. I feel imprisoned in the wrong generation. It is inevitable that you will tire of me. All such affairs testify to that. I have been interned in a small flat here beside the theatre. All night I lie awake (as now), afflicted by the sound of two people having sex next door, with a baby crying in the same room. Why is overhearing sex so primitively disgusting when it can, if it is right, be so beautiful? Each time I hear them, I feel like weeping. Victoria. You. Me.

I might as well tell you a little more about her. It is easier to write than to say it. When I try to describe her, I am distracted by your sweet face and by my guilt. But you need to know. Exactly what I feel.

There is no doubt that Victoria is beautiful. She has the kind of beauty which does not diminish with age. She becomes more elegant each year, more distinguished. She is a woman who, even in our early love, seemed emotionally complete. One was proud of her and the fact that she lacked vulnerability was somehow a relief. It left me free to get on. I like vulnerability in a woman, but when I married I was so busy that I hadn't the time or the desire (lazy, I know) to nurse a relationship. It had to be simple. And simple it was. Or perhaps Victoria spotted that fact and made it simple. As I say, she is clever.

Now . . . now, what? There is something about her beauty that is atrophied. The fact that it, she, we don't grow or change makes me feel that being together is pointless. It is like having an exquisite painting in the room, but it is just that, a presence that animates feelings of admiration but with whom there can be no real communication. It would, however, be missed were it to disappear. Please, my love, try not to be hurt by that last sentence. It is the truth, as far as I understand it.

The more important thing is that there is something deeply raw and incomplete about you, Dorcas. Something to discover. I don't mean that you are to be pillaged and found out. I mean that you are open and volatile and tender. You move me. Literally, make me feel I am moving again. I should sleep now. This letter will upset you: the fact that I don't talk of my marriage as if it is over and that I do not make you any promises. The trouble is there is something absolutely fixed about it, while, as I say, with you, there is constant movement. If I am honest, I suppose I need both, but . . . But . . . I'll leave what comes after that 'but' to a conversation not a letter. It is an important 'but'.

Bless you my sweet Dorcas. Soon I will see you. With love,

    J

*

The baby was in my arms. Every time I hold a baby, I wonder if I could manage to have one myself. The answer up until the Armistice was yes. Yes, I don't see why not. All the usual bonuses: softness of skin, feeling of belonging, comfort, little toes, those baby fingers, long eyelashes, trusting, entirely lovely, a bit heavy but manageable. Come the Armistice and all hell broke loose. The baby started bawling. I made for the door but Nina motioned me to stay and shot on with her journey like a racing driver. 'I've started, so I'll finish . . .' *Wham!* 'And the government announced' – *neeow*, accelerate round a corner – 'a break to . . . and all the men . . . and all the soldiers . . . and it was all . . . but that's not where it ends, you see, straight after,' – here, her thoroughness fought with her baby's hunger – 'straight,' – scream – '*straight* after the end of the war,' – bloodcurdling yell . . .

'Oh, James,' she said, as she took the bundle from me and jiggled him up and down. I thought how nice it would be if she got out her breast and fed him there and then in front of the girls. They would have remembered that. Instead, she toodle-pipped us and slipped out on her macaroni-thin legs to the privacy of her office.

I found it amusing that the child was called James. There is something childish behind the eloquent wording of your letter, I realise, as I re-read it now. A child crying out that it is doing something wrong but can't help it. Stamping its foot, its foot that is rooted in the quiet life. And yet the frankness of it had touched me at the time, as your frankness always does.

'So, was that useful?' I asked the girls when Nina had gone and I walked round to see what they had written down about the war. Result? One exchange of notes about the school bus, a pair of scissors denoting battle with Germany and the names of four countries, misspelt.

'Now, how are you going to remember anything she said if you didn't write it down?'

'She went too fast.'

'So? You could have done a few mind maps.'

'But Miss Trevelyan, everyone's always saying do mind maps. And *everyone* goes too fast.'

Suddenly I felt sorry for them. The whole school day is like that. This, that, the other, this again and back to that. I looked at their faces in the way I had hoped Tanya would look at mine. And I saw through their eyes to brains contracted by speed and pressure. But with some effort I retained the teacher's pose.

'Well, you should have got *something* down. You should always take notes. Especially when the inspectors come.'

'Oh, the bloody inspectors,' one of them rightly roared. And I started to giggle.

'Yes, the Battle of the Inspection. Write it down. Go on, quick, quick, quick, write it *down*. Write spelt w-r-i-t-e not r-i-g-h-t, right?'

*

46

Oh, the *slowness* of Neville. We would still be at the first stile if he had been in charge.

'You see that tree.' (Remember, Kenneth Williams, nasal.)

'Yes, I do see that tree.'

'Well, if you look at it carefully, you can make out a woman holding a large child. Can you see that?'

No.

'And the child is so large that the woman has a humped back. Can you see that?'

No.

'Oh, come here. Dorcas, come here. Have you always been called Dorcas, by the way? It's a strange name, isn't it? If you look from this angle—' (Remember slow, all very slow.)

'Yes, if you look from that angle,' I interrupted, 'you can see an ape's bum defecating, and I have always been called Dorcas, yes.' Then I felt so bad that I suggested we sit down and have our picnic. 'Which was the picnic by the way, (a), (b) or (c)?' I asked.

'I can't remember,' he said glumly.

'This is lovely fruit cake.'

You are much better than me at teasing, Jamie. Remember this time? I go: 'Why shouldn't men wear shorts in the summer?'

You: 'Men should never wear shorts in public, and *you* shouldn't wear Lycra.' I was standing in your kitchen in a Lycra top, of the kind I wear at the gym.

'Please,' you said calmly, 'never wear Lycra anywhere

near me, I can't stand that stuff and you look silly in it in any case.'

'Do I?'

'A bit.'

'Well, it's better than the shorts that you wear *in private.*'

'Well, when I do wear shorts, I hide my legs under the desk so that even I can't see them.'

Me in battle mode: 'Oh, and when you get up to collect one of your hundred little morning snacks, you leave your legs behind so that you won't have to look at them walking into the kitchen?'

'Exactly. Now do be quiet. I can't concentrate with you chatting on like that.'

How lovely it is arguing with you. The satisfying sound of a wet towel being slapped about: slap, slap, slap. And everything cool and invigorated afterwards.

'Shall I tell you how I made the fruit cake?' Neville asked.

'Oh do,' I said, still sorry about the ape's bottom under which we were seated.

'Well,' he began, 'you get a bowl. I use a plastic bowl . . .'

I won't go on. He did though, for twenty-five minutes. That's the entire first half of WWI in Nina-time. When he had finished, he said, 'I'm sorry, I know I'm a bore. It's just that I like doing things properly and also I'm rather shy.'

'Yes, of course,' I reassured him. 'I'm shy too. Everyone's shy. Don't worry. Tell me about your job.'

'Well,' he said. 'My mother died of cancer a year ago so I have no relations left. I belong to a rambling group and I used to be a Christian but it didn't really work.'

'Oh, I'm sorry. Work though?'

'Well, religion seemed pointless.'

'I agree,' I said. 'But your job. Do you work?'

'Yes, I write exam papers.'

'What subject?' I asked and, with a sudden desperation for beauty, visualised a pair of green handmade shoes I had recently seen advertised in a magazine.

'Chemistry.'

I smiled.

'Alone? Do you work on your own?'

'Yes, all on my tod.'

The picture, already full of wallpaper and tupperware, now had an additional supply of examination board syllabi stacked chronologically on a flesh-coloured mantelpiece. I held on to the advert for the green shoes.

'Do you mind if I take my shoes off now?' he asked. I looked at him astonished. 'My feet are hurting.'

'Of course not. Just keep them out of the fruit cake perhaps?'

I felt him flinch like a nervous dog. His feet could have been worse, as it happened, but the angle they sat at was so very stupid that I couldn't help staring at them.

'They've always been like that,' he said. 'They tore my mother's skin when they were born.'

'Oh, how awful. So you came out feet first?'

'I did, yes.'

This was becoming unpleasant. Or rather, I was, yes, it was me who was becoming unpleasant. And I realise now that I was enacting it all as if you were the amused audience. I thought my being unkind would appeal to you. Where did I get the idea that only a woman with edge is worth exploring? Particularly when you say you like me for my benevolence.

I keep coming back to the first evening you visited, how we went straight to bed. There was no question in my mind as to whether or not we would sleep together, though how and to what degree I had no idea. Each move, fruit cake to walk to stile to crashingly boring tour round an accidentally-fallen-upon stately home, involved, with *Neville*, a long discussion. With you, about that most important of matters, we needed no discussion.

Ah, but we did. I remember now. We talked of it in one of our early phone calls before the comic series of conversations conducted from Cologne.

'I'd like,' I said slowly, 'I'd like to find another language for sex. I mean . . . I mean, it's like religion in a way, sex. The language, even the act itself, in both areas, is sullied. Don't you think? I have this feeling that there's something underneath which remains unspoilt, which isn't a copy or a fake.'

'We're all animals,' you said, 'but I recognise what

you are saying and I have thought it myself in some way.'

As I recall those measured words, I see that your mind was not on what I was saying but on the practical implications of our sexual activities. Unfaithfulness. I was describing the religion of sex and you were thinking of betrayal. So why did we go to bed so fast, Jamie? Why, if you were so worried? Answer me that. For me, it was inevitable and also innocent. I knew we were meant to and yet 'meants' are spiritual. They have their less generous equivalents in the law courts. Perhaps at that moment it was God who presided over us, a god who thinks beyond the practical ways in which we organise our lives.

Then there was another complication. In bed, you turned to me and stroked my hair. 'I'm not an old man but I've an old man's trouble. It takes me time,' you said.

'What does that matter?' I said, touching your face.

'It matters a great deal.'

'Not to me. It doesn't to me.' And it didn't. And it never has. And it still doesn't. Partly, and only partly, because we overcame it and were, by force of circumstance, made to create our own language.

You were reluctant even to kiss then, as if kissing, not penetration, were the most intimate of acts. What *did* we do then? I remember only the fact that I knew how to proceed and felt not a moment's hesitation, that I touched every part of you and smelled you with the pleasure, yes, of an animal finding not just its mate but its own pack again.

'What lovely hands you have,' you said sleepily.

I knew it to be true, only because I knew what I could say with them, things I couldn't say with words. And I wanted to tell your body how much I respected the way it had aged before its time, how much I loved the rise of your stomach, the lovely, soft roundedness of your arms. But none of these separately. It was the entirety of you lying there on my bed, receiving my fingers, which I instantly loved.

And how funny you were. 'I think,' you had said, 'that a bowl of fruit would be nice.' And so there it was, in the bedroom. A little still life on the chest of drawers. 'I'd like a grape,' you said. So noble.

The next day, after we had made love in the beginnings of our own way, you were very quiet. And a little restless. Now I see it was because you are confused in other people's houses (see the above rendition of your 'my own room' soliloquy) and don't know quite where to put yourself. In addition, we had not quite found the right way to talk to each other, but I liked it that you didn't try to combine chat with touch. I remember you just sitting; sitting and sitting, then rubbing your eyes. Now and then I approached and glanced my hands over your face and you accepted that with an embarrassed but pleased reluctance. This awkwardness, which was not shyness but in fact a strength, a self-containment, an interest in rhythm, had tremendous charm. Recently, you had taken up the piano, you said, and I imagined you moving through the lines of music in the same way, slowly but with determination, then speeding up, making a mistake, stopping, starting again. I know now that you are a man who does not like or believe in short-cuts.

All day, both new to these duets, we played, side by side, occasionally jostling each other. But by four in the evening, I could see you were brewing a worry.

So I took you to a concert.

We sat on hard chairs on a raised platform and joked unkindly about the conductor in his white tails. 'Terrible,' you said gently, in a way that told me if ever you met him, you would be kindness itself. Then you folded your hands in your lap again, a gesture I love in you, a sign of the decorum which I so often lack. I felt awkward. Some of the performers were my pupils and, though I was fond of them ordinarily, tonight they seemed gangly and stupid, extending themselves too far so that one felt in their performance all the pain and boredom they had endured during rehearsals for the past six weeks.

I should have taken you home at the interval. But some impulse, not to punish (later, you said it was that), but to endure a thing to the end forced me to stay and you with me. I knew your back was aching, and that throughout the second half you were thinking of Victoria.

*

'Guess what, girls?' I said to the First World War group. 'I've got a DVD that tells us all we need to know.' I had pinched a documentary from the drama department. 'So Nina combined with visual stimulation should drum it in. Yes?'

'Why didn't you get the DVD before she did that lecture?' one Emma Forbes piped up.

'Because it would have been too easy,' I lied. 'You like everything easy, like a baby. Mouth open, dollop it in.'

'I don't. I've read *War and Peace*,' said Emma.

'All right, not you then, but most people like it easy. And not just children. Frankly, I'm as bad. And anyway, actually, as a matter of a fact, I didn't know we had the DVD.'

'So, as I said,' you resumed, 'it will be very difficult. Everything's against it. We'll have to lie. Do you want to be complicit in that?'

No, I didn't want to lie, but the irony was that its very difficultness was one of its chief attractions. I *wanted* it to be difficult. Everything important is difficult. I wanted *you* to be difficult too. Not unfair, but exacting. Which indeed you are. And, in addition, I had and still have the distinct feeling that our love would not involve lying but telling the truth. I wonder now, looking back on my life, if I have ever really told the truth. I wanted to, but . . .

On the way back to London, on the last morning of

that first stay at my house, once more you placed your fingers gently around the back of my neck as I drove you to the station. As if you knew that this journey (not to mention the bigger journey on which, as I said before, we had tacitly embarked) was as hard as the first, only differently so. I didn't crunch the gears this time. When you have been intimate with a person's body, you no longer crunch the gears. Instead, I cried because I knew you would not kiss me. 'We say goodbye here,' you had announced just inside my front door. 'Understand? After that, we just go. It's the only way I can manage. I'm a very private person, Dorcas.'

For a terrible moment, I thought Mr Eighteenth Century was going to proffer his dry lips. He had lip-salved them regularly throughout the day. ('I've just got over a cold.') We were seated in the marquee.

'However did we get *here*?' I said, suddenly joyful at the oddity of the day and more so at the fact that surely, *surely* it would come to an end soon and I would be back at home and telephoning the green shoe man.

'Accident,' he said, shrugging his shoulders so emphatically that he nearly crushed his earlobes. How exhausted he must be by nightfall if all his actions involved such exaggeration. 'Pleasant though, isn't it – the sun, the tea, the walk.' And he stretched his head forward. It's coming, I thought, and retracted into a coughing fit, which was, in fact, genuine. A piece of cake had gone down the wrong way. I had to get it out, which I did. It landed on Neville's collar.

'I'm so sorry,' I heaved.

'Never mind,' he said, opening his mouth wide and retrieving it as if for his own consumption.

Well, that was it. Either he was deliberately trying to put me off or nerves had sent him off his rocker. Knowing it to be the latter, my mind dished up an unsavoury series of images of myself in similarly uncontrolled states and yet thinking, as he probably was just then, that I was being funny. I had to go home. That very minute. Neville was becoming a mirror into which I had no desire to look.

My darling Dorcas,

I want to thank you for the way in which you helped me the night before I left your house. You were so generous. You asked nothing of me and yet gave so much of yourself. I caught a glimpse of myself in that rather unfortunate long mirror you have at the bottom of the stairs and thought, why ever is she interested in me? But then I have never liked mirrors. (You seem to?) In any case, my love, you must understand that I am an ingrained cynic. History tells us, as I warned you in my letter from France, that relationships between two people of such different ages as ours cannot last. Three years perhaps, five at a stretch, but longer than that and it becomes a trial to the younger one and a source of fear to the older one. Added to which, my circumstances . . . But I must get all this out of my head for the moment and relish what you have given me. I have found that I do not exactly know what that is until we have been parted for a few days.

Thank you for your loveliness.

J

I don't know how I could have thought that a maker of green shoes should be in on a Saturday but there was something in the style of the particular pair I had seen in the advert that suggested dedication. So, on my return from my outing with Neville, wanting loveliness and being impatient, I made my call.

'Hello.'

'Hello.'

'Is that Johnnie Redfield?'

'Redfield here.'

'I saw some of your shoes in a Sunday magazine, forget which, which, er, which I liked and wondered if you could tell me how you go about ordering them and I liked that business of them being made for each customer but was confused by the note about fifty pounds deposit. I'm sorry to bother you on a Saturday.'

'That's all right. I live shoes,' said Mr Redfield.

'Really?' I cheered up. I was right about Mr Redfield being dedicated.

'Yes. Where did you say you saw the advert?'

'In a Sunday magazine, forget which. Sorry. Thanks.'

'And what were you after exactly?'

'As I say the green shoes that were in the magazine.'

We spent fifteen or twenty minutes discussing the shoes, how they were made, how it was vitality not high heels that made a woman sexy ('my own view at least'), how as a teacher ('What of?'; 'English.') I did an awful lot of running about and needed better shoes than I could buy off the shelf.

'You're absolutely right,' Mr Redfield said. 'People don't appreciate the importance of footwear. I don't mean just in their ordinary everyday lives, but in *history*.'

'How do you mean, in history?' I sighed, willing to continue with the conversation only because there was hope of a parcel at the end of it.

'Well, take, for example, Napoleon's retreat from Moscow in the winter of 1812.'

'What about it? I'm rubbish at history.' (And I wanted a bath.)

'Thousands of his soldiers died from the cold. Now, if they'd had better footwear, appropriate for the conditions, many of them would have survived and he'd have ended up better off. History might have been different. He might have won at Waterloo. Historians pay no attention to the effect of podiatry on the outcome of events.'

'Podiatry? Well, I'm teaching First World War poetry this term.' I rallied myself. 'That was a terrible war, wasn't it? Would footwear have improved matters then, do you think?'

'Of course. What were many soldiers who spent weeks and weeks in the trenches hampered by? Trench foot. If they'd had appropriate footwear they'd have been OK, there'd have been less suffering, not so many invalided back to Blighty, and the war would have been different.'

'I see. You mean, if Hitler had worn better shoes instead of those jackboots he might have won?' (The bath was now run.)

'It's possible.'

'I must say, from what I've heard about him he was very cantankerous, wasn't he, all that bellowing in his speeches. Maybe it was caused by his boots pinching?'

'It isn't beyond the bounds of possibility.'

'Actually, I was in the vicinity of Winston Churchill's statue today' – Mr Redfield's diction was catching – 'and I particularly noticed his feet. His shoes seemed quite comfortable. Maybe that's why we won and Hitler didn't. Do you think?'

'I haven't got that far yet.'

'Sorry, what?'

During the course of Mr Redfield's next speech, I poured oil into the bath and was soothed by watching the patterns it made on the surface of the water.

'I'm researching a book on the history of footwear. I'm only up to the Anglo-Saxons. They had pretty shoddy shoes, I must say. But the thing is, I'm good at the research but seem unable to write well. You say you're an English teacher. Do you think we might co-operate, me researching the subject and you writing what I tell you? I can see you're interested in the subject. Could I take you out to dinner, perhaps, and discuss the proposition?'

'No! I mean, sorry, thank you, but the thing is, just at the minute, permanently in fact, I have too much mark-ing to do, and then there's reading the set texts, and keeping up with all the form-filling, not to mention meetings after school, Year Eleven outings to the the-atre, et cetera et cetera. I honestly don't think I have time or could live up to your expectations. So shall we just decide about delivery of my green shoes, which we both hope will improve my podiatric (was it?) health and mobility? If you don't mind, that is.'

'Yes, yes, of course. I'm a terror when it comes to the history of footwear, which is a little different from podi-atry by the way. My wife is always complaining about it. She even threatened to divorce me when I was on the Celts.'

Enveloped in hot water, I managed a smile and an attempt to impress upon Mr Redfield my urgency, telling him I would send the required diagrams of my feet *immediately* and a deposit of fifty pounds, and thus eliciting a final agreement from him that they would arrive in a few months 'as I've got a new kind of suede on order'.

'And you have to take into account my long toes.'

'Exactly.'

Having dispensed with Mr Redfield, I thought I'd get shot of Neville at the same time. So one more phone call, thankfully just a monologue this time as Ms Bright Lights was out.

'Hello Tanya, it's me, Dorcas. Just to say – I'm sorry to be rude but – Neville was awful. Sorry. Thanks. Goodbye.'

Psychology

'I'm not afraid to be watched,' said Ursula, the head of psychology, the head of herself as it happens, there being only her in the department.

'We can see that,' sneered Pork. Ursula was bending over her sun lounger in a thong.

'I don't mean it in that way. I mean by the inspectors.'

'I'm sure they'd love poking about in your department,' Pork went on. 'They might not hear a word you said, though, if you were dressed like that. Not that that matters, they'd go away with anal retention either way.'

'Piss off,' said Ursula nastily.

I listened to this banter with a feeling of discomfort. I knew that Ursula and Pork had slept together ('I'm not being funny, but this is a secret, Dorcas. Got it?') and I found it unsettling that they were being so unpleasant to each other. ('I thought she was a lesbian anyway?' I said. 'She varies,' he replied.)

I was so shy that day on the beach – a sixth form outing – that I stayed in my 'frock'. I didn't want the staff, least of all Pork, inspecting my body. The sea was far out and I could change near the water, taking one of the girls with me as a chaperone. This particular girl – a comfortingly large figure – and I bounced up and down in the waves, trying to find a bit of surf, while she informed me that she had just broken it off with 'Dean', and was going on a holiday where everyone dresses up as Vikings and lives like Vikings for a week without washing. I felt very fond of her and loved her for her simple warmth as well as her eccentric hobbies. I did not inquire what Dean had done wrong. It is a rule not to ask.

Coming out of the water, I wanted to read. The days had been so full of meetings and I was so missing talking to you that I longed to be on my own, away from the crudity and gossip that comes always of a group of staff off duty in the sun.

One day in your flat, you had given me a book list. 'At Cambridge and not read Proust, not read Philip Roth, not read Colette?'

'I read *English* Lit,' I parried, knowing you liked to go on about Cambridge because you had been one of its scholars.

I don't remember what I was reading that day, but I know I couldn't concentrate. On one side of me were the sixth formers, huddled together smoking, a little below them the staff. In the end, I submitted to the pull of the staff, picked up my book and straw bag and joined them. Ursula was in full swing about one or another of St Edmund's' systems that she considered facile. I lay there feeling prissy in the 'frock' with its navy blue flowers.

'Anyway,' she said, 'I'll tell the inspectors about my cluster group and that will shut them up about me being a single-handed department.'

'Ooh, single-handed,' joked Pork. 'What's happened to Randall then?'

'Piss off!' (Oh, tiring! Oh, bad taste. And who was Randall?)

I had considered cluster groups of local English specialists myself and thought I should begin one, but couldn't be bothered with organising all the invitations and the biscuits. I started to quiz Ursula on hers and all of a sudden, relieved of Pork's obscenities, she became uncharacteristically pleasant.

'Come and join us. We're having a meeting sometime next term. You can see how a cluster group works.'

And this, my dear Jamie, is where the inspection of the male species, which, up to this point had been merely an embarrassing nuisance, became a little more complicated.

After my acid call, Ms Bright Lights kept her distance for the entire summer holiday. But it was after that when I was dished up someone by Ursula herself.

Ursula is a great fan of *life*. She's one of those people

who insistently places it in your vision when you are just settling down to watch something pleasantly mind-numbing on TV, as if to say, stop doing that and climb Mount Everest. Unless you climb Mount Everest *now*, this absolute *minute*, you're wasting your life, your heart, your soul, your brain . . . And so on and so on and so on, until you give in and say, all right, I'll shoot myself. Will that satisfy your thirst for drama?

'Hi, Dorcas. Great you're here,' she said, as I arrived at the cluster group meeting. She was dressed with considerably more style than at school where tights with leopard spots were not unknown. 'This is Randall.'

'Hello,' I said (still shy). 'Are you a psychologist too?'

'Oh no, get me *outta* here,' he boomed in his American treacle voice, big hands raised in a position of dominant surrender.

'He's my new boyfriend,' said Ursula, as if emerging him from a posh carrier bag. (How anyone has the confidence to claim anyone as either new or their own beats me.)

The cluster group turned out to be more informal than I had expected. A brief chat over a drink in the pub, from which I learnt nothing. And then dinner in the adjoining restaurant.

'This place is famous for witchcraft,' announced Ursula, swilling down the last of a pint of beer. 'Apparently, people who come here usually go away under a dark cloud of supernatural influence.'

Show off.

'Nice,' I remarked, feeling uneasy. I often feel hyper-sensitive in pubs and restaurants, but I was a gaping hole in this place.

'Sit next to Lawrence,' said Ursula. 'He'll look after you.'

It was probably said kindly, but when vulnerable, one hates to have it pointed out. (You are boring and now you are vulnerable.)

'So, you're a St Edmund's girl too, are you? Smart little get-up,' said Lawrence and winked. Then he opened both eyes wide and stared. I rather liked his eyes. They sort of crossed over in a way that, if a Mr Eighteenth Century affliction, would have been the confirmation of mental illness but on him were an accessory of the highest quality. Gleaming tie-pin eyes.

'My dress, you mean? I bought it last week.'

Why the blazes I said that, I don't know. It just came out as things often can when one is in the company of the charming.

'I meant the school actually, but I like the dress. Good colour.'

'School is school,' I said looking into my wine.

'Don't you like it much then?' he asked invitingly.

I realised that, oddly, no one has ever asked me that question in quite that way, and rarely have I allowed myself to ask it either. I was brought up to accept circumstances, never to fight or abandon them. With a pay slip arriving every month, the notion that there might be something else I could be doing seemed merely de-stabilising. I told him I did like it.

'Not convinced,' he said, pointing his fork at me, tipped by two cubes of melon, with which it looked as if he was about gently to wipe my face clean of its deceptive mask of enthusiasm. 'What else do you do?' he went on.

'What, you mean *hobbies*?'

'Yes, if you like, hobbies.' (Oh, here we go again.)

'Yoga, um, swimming, um, reading...'

'Yes, yes, but what about you? Really about *you*. Tell me,' he said tenderly.

Tell me, oh tell me. How I love those words and yet always find them a touch obscene. Tell me, show me, all mixed up with 'tell me where you hurt'. You never say 'tell me', Jamie. You want to know, but you do not inquire in that direct way. You simply wait for me to say. I can sense you are waiting, but you never urge yourself upon me. Instead, you are silent, make a space inside yourself to contain whatever it is that is worrying me. Then when I am ready, I walk over to you and say, 'Jamie, what exactly does buildings and contents insurance actually cover? I mean, milk spillages, drunken brawls, burst pipes...?'

'Ah, that.'

And we deal with it quietly. Or else those other lovely times when we have set ourselves an agenda: my teaching, your teaching, our love and where it is going and always, calmly but necessarily, Victoria.

I feel my way carefully. I desperately want to know what she looks like, all about her, but this is your private business and it is wrong to pry or draw comparisons. You struggle. I am silent. We can only take this topic slowly. Even though we have spoken about it several times and you sent that letter about it from France, the ground still hasn't been anywhere near fully covered.

I love it that you neither force one out of oneself nor shift yourself too fast either. You are not a manipulator. Oh, Jamie. Rare gift. The whole world seems to push one way, while you stand still and straight and wait.

Lawrence stared again, his bright eyes sliding off at diagonals. 'You're complicated, aren't you?' he said.

'It may just be that I'm trying to talk about myself in a noisy, crowded pub,' I said defensively.

'No, I don't think it's quite that, is it? It's more that you are about to enter a transition and you're nervous.'

Had he not been in possession of, in addition to the athletic green eyes, a pleasantly solid chest and a remarkably handsome face, I would have fobbed him off. One thing I dislike in both men and women, particularly as it happens in women, is intrusion, by which I mean an assumption that more is known about one than one knows oneself. But he was, in fact, gentle with his probing and also artful.

The teacher opposite, a late-middle-aged woman who looked as if she took holidays in the south of France and had a husband who wore sports jackets, was talking about a book she had read called *Hindu Attitudes Towards Masturbation*. If it hadn't been her speaking, I would have giggled, but it was a psychology meeting, I suppose, and she was the kind of person who made silly things sound sensible. Lawrence detached himself from me deftly and said, 'Gracious, I thought the Indians were fiercer than Calvinists on that topic, but then I suppose the *Kama Sutra* . . .' His left eye drifted towards his right.

I quietly chomped on an avocado salad, grateful for the respite, but I was aware that I wanted him back again. I feel awkward telling you this, Jamie. But it is how it was. Perhaps I was in need of that sort of solicitude, but only for an evening, a couple of evenings. I became vain then, and was glad I had been to the steam bath before the meal. It had made my face glow. Well, it had glowed when I had looked at it in the mirror two hours earlier. It could well have changed since. It is, I can objectively say, a face that is one hundred per cent unreliable, inconsistent and downright disloyal.

Like yours. How funny your face is in this respect. Deep down, I'm not at all sure you were not made for celibacy. Sometimes after we kiss at length (kissed, kissed, why can't I put it in the past tense?), bags as big as pillows appear under your eyes. And then you have something to eat, tuck in your denim shirt and behold, the bags are gone.

There are things I can tell you here that I could not quite manage to say to you in person, however honest we promised to be. And one of them was my worry (it must also have been yours) that each time I saw you after too long a space of time, I would no longer desire you. I hate the cruel side of sex. I neither understand nor do I want it. Perhaps God engineered the lapses between our meetings in order to avoid the horrifying moment of boredom that had crept up on me in every other relationship I had had, and usually sooner rather than later.

With you. No. Never. Never once, on your arrival, did I feel anything other than pleasure and relief. Pleasure that you smelled of lamb chops still. It's true, that lamb-ish smell was the best. And relief that you were somehow always ahead of me. Self-deprecating in the extreme and yet fixed in your strength:

'How are you feeling?'

'Me? Not sure really.'

'Your play going well?'

'Play? Not very. It's got no bite.'

'Body feeling good?'

'Body? Not bad. Need a bit more exercise.'

That loveliest of poets, Samuel Taylor Coleridge, once wrote that friendship is the shade of a tree. You were that. But you were also my lover.

Lawrence turned back to me. 'Do you know what you need?' he said, rather than asked. 'You need to be treated.'

'I already go to a homeopath,' I said, knowing exactly what he meant.

'No, no, be given some treats. Taken out.'

'Oh, it's just that I've got a rather small face. People always say that to people with small faces.'

'No, it's not that,' he went on.

'Well, in that case, yes please,' I snapped. 'I'd like the following: while we're on the face, I'd like a facial every fortnight, and then a new Hoover, mine's stopped picking stuff up, a secretary, a new bathroom, a long holiday, one of those colour stylists, you know, who comes into your house and fills it with green because you need a—'

'Don't joke,' he said, touching my arm (nice). Oh Jamie, he was delicious, as well as a little disgusting. Do you understand the combination? I can hear you saying, 'We-ell, in a way,' in that lovely hesitant voice you use when you don't really understand at all but are willing to accept that there are more philosophies in heaven and earth than Professor Loring has dreamt of.

'Dorcas, I'm talking deeper than that,' he crooned.

'Oh yes, all right then,' I said. 'All right, can I have *very* deep then? A lovely man with a big You-Know, who isn't insistent, but is passionate, dematerialises when I'm busy, turns up only when I'm not and et cetera. '

'So you are single then?' Lawrence asked gently.

'No!'

No. No. Since that moment, I could never say I was single.

That moment. That moment which existed and still does, outside the sequence of events as a self-contained episode.

You were seated on my sofa, a piece of curvaceous furniture you would never have chosen yourself, although it had generously contained me through many nights of sleeplessness when my bed felt too empty without you or my head too full of you. You were very tired and (do not dispute this), I had just knelt between your legs and said to you, 'I can't go on with this. It hurts too much. We are being unwise, not to mention unkind. You were right the first time, Jamie. Victoria, I mean. When you said it would be too difficult.' You were silent. You could not deny it, you *had* said it yourself, but you did not want to hear yourself saying it again.

You kept your eyes closed and stroked my hair as I knelt. Oh so good. So casual and yet tender and troubled.

'I'm exhausted,' you mumbled. And that said, you were expecting nothing and nor was I. Besides, I didn't know what I was doing.

('How much comes out?' I had asked a girlfriend once, on a coach journey together in Spain as fourteen-year-olds. 'Seriously, how much? Spoonful? Cupful? Jugful? Really, *tell* me. I want to know.' My friend had shrieked and some lads behind hooted, but I persisted. 'You don't mean *more*? You don't mean a pintful? You do, you mean a pintful, don't you?')

Most other acts of love I had performed, as far as I know, though the published repertoire seems to increase daily if spam emails are anything to go by. However, this simple action which is common to the most casual of schoolgirl romantic encounters I had been unable to perform, and I knew little of its mechanics. But my fingers, perhaps educated by two nights of contact with your very soft skin – crinkled chamois skin – my fingers knew how to begin.

I undid your belt. You sorted out the button at the top of your trousers, which is always so hard to deal with. And I brought out your cock. Small, soft, weary cock. It made me feel both tender and aroused at the same time. It flopped and yet I did not feel in the least inclined to laugh at it. Only with it, into it, on to it.

Suddenly my mouth found its way to you. This was the first time. Through all the hours I had lain with you I had not felt drawn to do this. But now, holding you in my mouth, it was the most peaceful feeling I have experienced since – when? Since *when*? A destination. A home. A mothered feeling and yet also so intensely exciting that it made me move myself on you, your leg between my legs, as I held you. That skin, such a particular texture, taut but soft at the same time. How lovely, how respectful, how poignant this is, I thought. But then instantly, without warning, my body stole all my thoughts and made its own statement.

Despite the no to Lawrence's question about being single, a few weeks after the cluster supper he still came to my house. In fact, my no was the perfect answer for a man like Lawrence because he knew that, in a moment of hurt and mutual flattery, it meant yes.

And here is another brutal truth. As he walked round the house, looking, smiling, picking up small gifts given to me by the children at school, I thought, This man would be much easier to live with than Jamie. He would go out a lot for a start. He would go out for days at a time to sort out teams of tired businessmen, and I would have the house to myself. Jamie, however, would park himself in a chair and sit for hours without moving, talking, anything, so one could not quite think of him as absent and certainly not as present either. And then, finishing a chapter and bored, suddenly just when I was launched into some good quality thinking, he would say, 'Kiss me.'

Professor Loring, lecturer and poet, would live by a routine that would involve my participation. Lawrence of psychology, on the other hand, would be relaxed, come and go, not be distressed if the lid was left off the marmalade. 'What does it matter? Who cares?' he'd say. Whereas you'd be put out, because details matter.

Which is why I love you. Because your soul is such that your body ensures, for its welfare, physical meticulousness.

'Nice little house. Let me take you to dinner, though.'

'But you've only just arrived.'

'Yes, but I want to treat you, remember?'

(The New Dorcas Dictionary. *Treat*: a single thing, an event without a past or future. *Moment*: a second that is emblematic of a whole lifetime.)

'Oh, all right. Thanks. Do I have to dress up?'

He shrugged, but I knew jeans wouldn't do, so went upstairs and threw some clothes about and found a pair of tight velvet trousers and a posh T-shirt. I didn't want to go out.

I began, at this point, by the way, to say the name in my head, with a French accent. I know French isn't your strong point, Jamie, but please, if you can bear to think of him at all, think of him as *Lor-ance*. It works better. In any case, *Lor-ance* had already booked dinner at a posh restaurant: tables far apart in a large ocean-sized ballroom, chandeliers, the lot.

'Does Madam have a coat?'

No, Madam doesn't. Nor does Madam have a handbag, nor does she have much idea of swish restaurant etiquette, nor does she know quite what to say.

'So,' said *Lor-ance*, leaning back in his chair. The little round table was so isolated it was like being on a boat (not one I should like to get married on either). I began to get that light-headed feeling that my homeopath has told me results from thinking about the future and not accepting 'where one is'. Quite right. I did not want to be here one bit.

Lawrence saw this and put his hand over mine and said, 'Relax, I won't eat you. Though it would be nice.'

'Would it?' I said, stupidly. 'What have you done to your finger?'

He lifted his hand and examined his forefinger, which was a nasty mess of dried cut and bruise. 'I was doing some DIY,' he said, 'and the hammer slipped.'

He then waggled the finger at me nastily, as if to say, now I'm just checking you for squeamishness, to see if you're the standoffish madam you seem to be. In order to be fully integrated, you need to tolerate a top French restaurant, immediately followed by fish and chips out of newspaper at my place, with work tools lying around. What he actually said was, 'I didn't have any plasters at home,' while using the injured finger to travel down the delicacies on the menu.

Apart from the finger, he was nice, attractive, admired by the waitresses and me alike. He ordered the food, then the wine and launched off on his questionnaire.

'So why don't you leave school then? You've got numerous talents. No ties.'

'I *have* got a tie. I *am* tied,' I asserted.

'Oh.'

'I told you I'm not single.'

'You seem very single to me.'

'But I'm not and I don't want to talk about it.'

Not any more than I *ever* wanted to talk about you. Do you remember that email I sent you one morning before school? I have it in front of me on my computer screen.

My darling Jamie,
You won't understand this perhaps, but I have just woken with a thought that hurts me, because it feels like a demand I cannot fulfil. And I want to tell you. The thought is – is it one all lovers have? – that apart from having to keep our love a secret because of Victoria, we should keep it a

secret for another reason. Because of what it is. I feel . . . I feel as if it is the kind of love that other people will want to destroy.

How can I say this in a way that will not sound to you like homeopathic claptrap? You are, as you keep reminding me, nineteen years older than me. You have told me several times that this is why it will end, but I was thinking this morning not of that, but of the newness we spoke of, that new language that is needed for sexuality. That's what feels vulnerable to me, not the age business. New things are always vulnerable. It is almost then our youth, certainly not your age, which puts us at risk. You know how frustrated you are that an idea you had many years ago has been copied and is now selling like hotcakes. It's a bit like that. That feeling that this newness will be copied, described, done by someone else and appear carelessly in some informal interview about marriage in a Sunday magazine.

I've told nobody about you. Not a single person. That's not like me and it's not because I'm embarrassed or ashamed but because I feel as if it can't be described or it will be spoilt. That's what I wanted to write to you about. The importance of secrecy. Do you see?

Dorcas

*

'What have you got to hide?' asked Lawrence, going at some smoked salmon.

'Oh, a great deal. Masses and masses. Or let's say things I'm trying to put behind me, which discussion doesn't help, because it puts them in front of me again.'

'Your lover is married.'

'Actually, I wasn't talking about that. I was referring to other things.'

'He *is* married.'

'Yes, all right, he is,' I said irritably. I was cross with myself for having mentioned you at all.

'Go carefully then. That can get very nasty. It seems fun at the beginning, but later, the complications—'

'Fun! It is *not* fun. I do not want *fun*.'

'Ah,' he said. 'I see. No fun.' As if I was unwell.

'So you've had complications then too? That's why you know?'

'Yes, once or twice,' he replied.

I somehow felt relieved at that. If done twice, it didn't resemble you and me. What had happened or half happened between us was distinguished by the fact that it was inimitable.

Seeing that he'd pushed me, Lawrence changed the subject, but, oddly, I floundered even more. As we talked about theatre and books and his work as a business consultant, I found myself realising that the only subject of conversation that really interests me is one that is centred on the two people seated opposite each other. To talk of other things strikes me as a lost chance. There is so much present within two human beings, which can be released if they like each other. Why divert?

At the end of the meal, Lawrence (remember: *Lor-ance*) looked up at me and said, as if suggesting an outing to the theatre, 'Dorcas, I would very much like to take you to bed.'

'I'm not a child,' I said. 'I can get into bed on my own.' He looked hurt. He'd said it so nicely too. 'Well, all right then, I'd actually like that very much.'

Jamie, deep down, I think paternalism was what I was attracted to in this man. And yet, it was also exactly what I resented.

News of *Lor-ance* spilled through the staff room and made those usually innocent breaktimes, when my urgent and conscientious attention is focused on flicking stationery catalogues into the bin, into times of embarrassment. Ursula was too clever to speak of it in my presence, of course. But I felt – as you know, my sensitivity is capable of verging on neurosis – that my standoffishness that day on the beach had made her want to push me into the same crude cattle market round which she jostled quite comfortably. And so she saw to it that everyone knew. And, my thankfully hidden Jamie, despite the fact that you had dismissed me and despite what happened next, this only served to strengthen the more sober, quiet, but deep love I felt for you. I wanted to protect you from all this, as if some part of you were inside me. I wanted to close your eyes to it, though, god knows, you have seen this kind of fiasco frequently enough, I am sure. But not with me in it, and I had entrusted myself to you.

However, you had rejected me. So I rebelled.

'So?' asked Lawrence.

'All right,' I said calmly, because it was exciting and because I wanted to find out. Yes, to inspect and be inspected. I was also drawn by his self-assurance, and the impression he gave that he knew me. I am not a great one for the 'I feel as if I have known you before' line of talk. But . . . I admit, I quite like it being said to me. It is, I imagine at least, like being a Freemason and feeling the folded finger of recognition in the handshake.

'Where?'

I was torn about that. On the one hand, I wanted the protection of my own home. In the middle of the night, when other people are sleeping, I can experience a child's terror in someone else's house. I do not like the process of learning the way round alien territory and dis-covering its unspoken rules. It is all right with an acquaintance, but, in this situation, I wanted nothing extra to concern myself with. At the same time, I did not want this man, this probing, charming man, in 'our' bed. But perhaps . . . perhaps, I concluded, cold-bloodedly, it would make a few things clear.

'My house.'

'Good,' he said, as if in his there were a pile of wash-ing-up or a black leather three-piece suite that would unnerve me.

We drove slowly, which I liked. Me giving directions. 'Just there . . . No, no, there. You've missed it.' And I realised, considering he had been there only hours before, that perhaps he too was a little nervous.

Standing in my sitting room, I said to him, 'Please don't tell Ursula. I mean she already knows, but please don't tell her this.'

'Oh. Ursula,' he said. 'I wouldn't tell her anything important. I know how she is.' And I suddenly thought, you've slept with her too. I nearly asked, but did not want it confirmed. I wanted this to be an experience that had no past. And no future.

When we reached the bedroom, we stayed there.

Jamie, I know you are going to say you want to hear exactly how it was. You have always been incredulous at my inability to remember serious sexual encounters. But you must understand, I genuinely *don't* remember them. All I know is that they have mostly been fast. And all I can say on this occasion is, we undressed ourselves and stood. Looked. I shuddered at the thought (a pre-vious memory returning) that he might take me to a mirror so that we could peruse ourselves side by side. But, fortunately, this was not the idea. Instead, he lay down and drew me down next to him where I instinc-tively fitted myself into the slightly plump side of his body.

'How long your neck is,' he said, stroking me. 'Pretty.'

Pretty is a word I dislike. I have a list of characters from books, all of whom are so pretty and so feckless and so the owners of small dogs (cf. Dickens) and so unintelligent. Pretty falls short of beautiful, falls short of anything important. I said nothing.

He shook me gently. 'I like you. That's what I mean. I like you very much.'

All right. Accepted. Nice. Moderate. Not overreaching.

From where I lay, I looked down at his cock, that stupid male organ, which has an ape-ish look about it and yet sometimes, in its activity, can be matched by nothing else in this universe. So this cock was sizeable and not handsome. But certainly reliable. It would get him to a station on time, win him a promotion, lead him the right way round a one-way system. Namely, give him confidence. I fingered it gently and his body wriggled with pleasure.

'That's nice. Thank you.' Then he turned on his side and kissed me, so that my arms were no longer free. There was a big tummy on him. One of those tummies that, under a jumper, makes you feel as if its owner might hand you a cheque for a thousand pounds, but naked, is well . . . is just a tummy.

'I want to give you pleasure,' he said, after the kiss. 'How would you like me to give you pleasure?'

I blushed. 'I have no requirements,' I said loftily.

'Come on. Don't be like that.'

'Really. I don't.'

'You mean you're giving me carte blanche?'

'Oh no, not that.'

'What then?'

Why all this talking? I thought. Handbook: *Chat gently to your partner about what they would like. Don't be selfish, but make your own needs clear also. Take it slowly.* Yes, yes, yes. But no, no, no.

You. Third, fourth, fifth stay, I do not remember. No romantic preliminaries. We tried, but they are time-consuming. I began to unbutton your shirt, but too slow, so you took over the job yourself and flung the thing to one side so that it landed half on the floor, half on the chair. (There's hope for me being careless with the marmalade lid, I thought.) And I too undressed myself. We had bookish ideas about undressing each other, but when it came to it we were too impatient. And so we fell on the bed with relief.

Home. Nakedness. Not at that moment sex, but home. 'You've put on a little weight. There.' And you stroked my thigh. 'Look, it's nearly as big as mine now.'

'No, it's not.' And I stretched it out to take a look.

'It is. Really,' you insisted. And we both held our legs in the air. 'And how are you?' I asked, lifting up your little cock, addressing it tenderly.

'Straining for you badly. Straining.'

'I think you've grown,' I said, stroking him. For he was a being in his own right, who needed much talking to.

'Not big enough yet,' you moaned.

'Well, I like him.' He was so pretty (pretty in the right way, the best way) when soft, so tiny and yet happy enough to enter and move inside me. And how elegantly you entered then, my feet on your shoulders. Not with that great masculine thrust, which I always find somehow vulgar and threatening, like someone doing shooting practice, but as if you were edging your way into me, finding me out.

'I want you to lose your mind,' you said.

'I don't believe in that. I want my mind.'

'No, really. I want you just to *feel*.'

'I do feel. I feel love.'

And I massaged your head, your hair, your back, your shoulders. Anything to show you. And you were so grateful. But you wanted me to feel something else.

Lor-ance, le maître. I could see he was a master, could feel it. Why was it then that I was so cruel both to myself and also to him?

'You have incredible vaginal muscles,' he said.

'Do I?'

'Fantastic. They should be patented.'

No thanks. But flattered, I clamped him. And the more I did that, the more he began thrusting. At first, I liked it.

Yes, size matters. And Lawrence knew it. But he was very heavy and all that questioning he had been doing so kindly ceased as his cock did the talking.

'Stop, stop,' I urged.

'Why?'

'Stop, please.'

And he did. This happened four times during the night.

'What is it?' he asked, not unkindly. He was just puzzled.

'I really don't know what it is. At a certain point, I want you to stop. It hurts and it's, well, sort of too harsh,' I lied. Well, not entirely a lie. It did hurt a bit, but that wasn't it. There was something else, which I did not fully understand myself. Something more important than size.

He lay with his gentle, intelligent face cupped in his hand, his torso close to mine. 'You need a bit of help perhaps.'

And I thought, Oh yes, please help, sweep me up and carry me through this strange business, pay the bill with your credit card as deftly as you did in the restaurant, lead the way through the mines of my subconscious with a torch on your head. I would have followed him. Really, I would. He seemed a good guide. But I am a person who is endangered by discipleship, especially when it involves a series of psychically medicinal shocks.

'And that help is not going to be from me,' he said,

and stroked my cheek. 'As I said, you're complicated.'
What he meant was: you're *too* complicated.

Ah, well.

But do you know what I really thought at that
moment? I thought: yes, I am complicated. But you are
too, and you don't want to face it. Jamie faces everything,
every up, every down, every mood, every sea-change.
Lawrence wanted it easy. Though I admit this thought
did not instil confidence sufficient to save me from the
humiliation of his early morning departure.

'Now,' said Our Headmistress in a lunchtime meeting.
'Please understand. It does not matter how long it is. I
have had short ones, long ones, ones this thick, A4-sized,
A5. It simply doesn't matter. Quality is what matters.'
Exactly, I thought, picturing your little fruit lengthening
in the night. 'Departmental handbooks each have their
own character. I shall, however, be issuing a checklist, so
that you can ensure that the essentials are included. But
remember, we *are* an independent school and we can do,
within limits, what we wish to do and what we believe
in.'

Exactly, I thought, recalling your admission that you
had once liked a young man. 'It depends on the context
in which you make your points,' she concluded. 'Context
is everything.' Correct again. And I thought of how you
explained that you had enabled, through your encounter,
the aforementioned young man to better love his wife
when he eventually married. 'But do protect with sticky-

backed plastic, or, well, just as it is, but use stiff material or it will be damaged through handling. Anyway, I don't need to go on. You know what I'm getting at.' Indeed . . .

The senior mistress looked peeved. She likes everything the same length, the same size, the same colour. Perhaps that's why her husband left her. Perhaps he was A5 white, instead of A4 pink.

Mathematics

Our Poor Headmistress. She was making earnest efforts to appease a staff half of whom slightly frightened her and the other half she itched to jolly up, take on a trip to Hobbs and encourage to buy some smart business wear. She herself had a penchant for clothes and could not understand the dismal taste of many of her colleagues.

'I'd like you to tidy up your displays,' she said during one morning break, as if it were only just then that she realised how cross she felt with many of us.

One of the chief culprits of messiness, both in the display and the dress departments, was Mrs Maud Scream, a maths teacher of twenty years' standing at St Edmund's, who wore big cardigans and looked like a nun in mufti. One could see that Our Headmistress found this stubborn little Scot a particular frustration.

'Tell Maud,' she said to the head of maths, a similarly

dusty type, keen on setting puzzles, 'to *do something* about her teaching room.'

I am not lying about her name, Jamie. And I relish it as I relish her. Yeats's lover was Maud, Tennyson wrote a poem called 'Maud'. A. S. Byatt has an elegant heroine named Maud. Maud, if said with a detachment from all grandmotherly associations, is a good, strong statement of a name (as is Dorcas). And as for Scream, well that was just one of those pleasant accidents, for (a) she *is* a scream and (b) her teaching does make you want to scream, as I discovered when I had her as the second on my list of colleagues to observe. She has a habit of rotating at speed round the classroom saying, 'No, I won't slow down. You have to catch up,' so that the children emerge jetlagged after sitting inert for too long in a speeding vehicle. Nonetheless, I always feel violent towards anyone who taunts her and have more than once surreptitiously removed a sweet wrapper stuck to the back of her cardigan when she has been standing in the lunch queue.

Her register, however, is as immaculate as Miss Shifter's. Not of the origami variety, but all filled in faithfully each night while (one imagines) her husband, Donald, stirs the stew made of last week's leftovers. She does, I have to say, look very much as if she herself is made of stew: stew hair, stew skin, stew skirt. And (unrelated but somehow connected in my mind) she falls asleep in most of the staff meetings.

'So,' Our Headmistress asks, 'what about Coral?'

'Very good.' 'Excellent.' 'Set well for the finishing line,' everyone choruses, as if betting on a horse. Then a silence and Maud, lifting her head, says slowly (remember: Scottish), 'She's not doing well for me.'

'But,' retorts our head of maths, 'you don't *teach* Coral, Maud.'

'Oh, don't I?' she replies, with such a delightful lack of self-recrimination that one cannot help admiring her. To the last man, in fact, she is loved. Even her considerable temper provokes only pleasure. She has such a firm aim that there is never any spillage of acid. And if there is, she wipes it up herself.

'What's the matter, Maud?' I asked her, shortly after she had shot the messenger and the head of maths had limped off, like an injured dog, back to his diagrams. ('She should tell me herself if she doesn't like my classroom displays.')

'Nothing is the matter,' she snapped. 'At least, it is nothing *you* need to concern yourself with, Dorcas, if I may say so.'

I felt ashamed then of my habit of collecting up seeds of gossip and scattering them wherever they'll take root and produce a little growth-spurt of therapeutic hilarity.

The thing about vulnerable, failing people is that they come off badly in initial meetings. They don't get jobs, they don't get picked up at parties, they don't get picked, full stop. But if, like Maud Scream, they are good, *good* people, if they have a long record of loyalty, that very vulnerability – no it is innocence – that *inno-cence* becomes the quality for which they are most loved. Beside me, as I sit in a café, there is a group of girls drinking smoothies. They are critical, brash, attractive and lamentably lack all of Maud Scream's deep-rooted qualities of patience and endurance. They go anywhere, any time, anyhow, lack any sense of moral direction at all, would make a pig's arse of origami and would doodle even on a public exam paper. Yet they shine with the confidence that is summed up in that obscene word they use in every other sentence: 'pull'.

'Who did you pull?'

'Shaun.'

'Who do you want to pull next?'

'Dave.'

'Oh, *him*? No-o-o, not him!' Screeches of laughter.

Whereas were Maud Scream to be seated in a café like this one (unlikely, but still), she would be a model of politeness.

And this is how I see her at home. She is leaning her head against an antimacassar, a pile of marked books in front of her, stew plates (from the supper table, which is laid straight after breakfast) all washed up, dried and put away by Donald (they have a rota). Maud is looking at a Damart catalogue she has studied every night for the past week: 'I think I *will* have this top. It would go well with my green skirt and my gardening trousers, would it not, Donald?' A postal order is sent. The parcel arrives. 'Och, Donald, I don't think this looks right at all. It's two inches too wide on the shoulders.' She folds it up, packs it up, walks to the post office, sends it off with a sharp, hand-written note inside, regarding the inaccuracy of Damart's measuring chart.

Tanya Wright's next delivery, courtesy of Bright Lights, was Alastair.

'I'm not sure,' says Tanya.

'Well, that could be a good thing, judging from—'

'Yes, yes, well, all right. I'll ask him to ring you, shall I?'

'What happened to the antlers that fell down when I visited you?' I stall for time.

'They're back on the wall, thank you. Right. Anyway, there's someone on the other line. Yes or no to Alastair?'

'Might as well try,' I say mournfully.

Try what, I thought? What am I trying to do? Sample every variety of man so that I can come back to you and say they are all better than you? Or all worse?

I decided not to think about it too much and now, a seasoned dater, forgot Alastair until he rang.

'We could, er, email for a bit first if you like,' he said.

'No, no,' I said, 'better get on with it. Jump in at the deep end.'

'I can't swim,' he said.

No reaction from me, though I sympathised with the gaffe.

'But yes,' he hurried. 'Yes, all right. Where?'

'Sorry, 'fraid that's your department. I'm a bit of a home bird. Don't know the pubs round here.'

'Well, er, what about The Grapes?' And we set off on the directions business again, right and left turns, roundabouts, makes of car, number plates, parking spaces.

When you and I arrived home after that delicate exchange about the soul (do you remember that conversation?), once more we knew what to do: music. Listen to some music. Mozart's piano concertos.

'I'm very keen on, er-er, Schubert,' said Alastair. 'And Beethoven's Fifth . . .' (something or other) '. . . but, to be frank, er-er, I prefer the, er-er, concerto in B minor to the symphony in A flat, but then there is the middle C one and the Germanic version also and the most recent, wonderful Alan Jones version.' (Or something.) 'And of course, er-er, Bartok is out, as is Rakhmaninov and Wagner and all the F sharp . . .' (something or others) '. . . especially violins, are not to my taste. There's nothing to match Mozart's serenade in G.' (Or F or something.)

Oh Jamie. *Please* come back. I had only just begun my music education. And even now, I can only remember bits of Haydn. And when I listen to that, I know we should be living together in a house where the only things that matter are books, silence, food, music, walking and bed. So now I don't listen to classical music at all except when I can't get to sleep.

'My aunt lives in, er-er, Lewisham,' Alastair went on, 'but she's thinking of a divorce.'

What's the connection, I wondered? Does Lewisham make one want to get divorced? Anyway, who cares about your aunt?

'My aunt's husband is a friend of mine. We often go on the, er-er, Eurostar together. It's a pleasant journey. Meal and half a bottle of good wine on the way, bit of shopping, straight back, another meal, the other half of the bottle as it were. Nice chap. And my mother, well, she's not too well. So I visit her on, er-er, Sundays. My aunt really thinks divorce at her age is impractical. I mean so many years totted up between them, too late to find someone else and so on. But she does struggle with Harry, though, as I say, I find him congenial. And one doesn't make friends like that at work much. You know, commute into, er-er, London, do the job, back home. I did go to Tanya Wright before and got on quite well. Met Diana. A decent woman, a bit Germanic, liked cleaning the bathroom and so on,' – here, Alastair screwed up his nose as if recalling smells of bleach – 'but also would go to bed at eight o'clock, so really our, er-er, *relations*, as they say in America, became limited.'

I tried to picture this rotund, decent looking man having 'relations'. I couldn't. I just couldn't. Well, when it comes to it, I can't imagine most people having 'relations'.

'By the time one got back from work and had had supper, it was at least eight, so really it was a bit of a, er-er, missed wicket.'

'Didn't you mention it to her? About the relations?'
'Er, no.'

Love doesn't add up at all. One and one doesn't make two when it comes to love. The poet Brian Patten was right when he called it a 'sick equation'. Poor Alastair. And poor Dorcas!

Example: when I visited you in Rome. We caught different planes there and back and took different taxis to the airport. And on the last morning, you were seated in the bedroom with your head in your hands. You thought I had gone, but I ran back to say goodbye a second time, a habit you dislike in women and people in general. (Me too, though I am more forgiving about it than you.) You could barely lift your head you were so tired. And I was tired too. I had rushed to the airport from school, rushed from the airport to your flat, rushed with you everywhere, desperate to see you. I had even drunk you for the first time in that little flat and both loved it and found it hard and strange. I was *tired*. My head was full of all the children from school, all the meetings that would happen in the next half of term, all the marking, all the everything. But one and one doesn't make two when it comes to love. Your head was fuller. Of what?

At the airport you avoided me. Walked smartly to one end of the concourse and hid behind the *Guardian* with a cup of coffee and a doughnut. I ran from one end to the other looking for you, bumping into people, my silly luggage swerving about on its silly wheels. Looking *everywhere* for that dear curly head of yours. But no. Lots of curly heads and none of them was yours.

When I finally did find you, I thought that might be the end of it. That is often the kind of irritation (unfair on the perpetrator) that can finish even the strongest of early loves. How clever you were about it. The way you switched the volume to zero until the swell of annoyance (which was only tiredness and guilt) subsided and your energy returned. And then you began to speak. And just as always, with us, your voice returned strengthened and different: I love you, love you so much. The 'so much' was the addition.

Will that happen this time? If I did not dare to hope that the same rejuvenation would occur, I would not be involved in this hateful dating scheme. I am only doing it for you.

'Well,' Alastair continued, 'Diana and I were together for two years, three and a half months. We jogged along quite, er-er, well. But then she decided to go back to Germany. So I signed on with Tanya again. Trouble is, she is rather hung up on the end result: er-er, marriage. I've done marriage. Don't see it's the most important thing. She makes you feel a relationship hasn't worked if the right result isn't reached. Just off the mark, a bit of companionship, as far as she's concerned. I suppose it mucks up her, er-er, figures. Anyway, um, what about you?'

I could think of nothing to say. Naught. So, instead, I

picked a book off the shelf behind me. We were in a pub whose walls were lined with books. It was like being in a library and I wanted Alastair to pull away from his endless accounts and feel himself to be here, in this pleasant high-ceilinged room.

'Listen to this,' I said, and read him a nonsense poem by Edward Lear.

'My aunt likes Lear. She's got a collection of his, er-er, verse. My mother reads it, but her eyes are defective. Increasing signs of cataracts and she's got that, whatever *is* it, that, er-er, condition?'

'Glaucoma?'

'That's it. So we get her those large print books. Very good system. A van comes round weekly. And I get free eye tests because of it. Because of the glaucoma.'

Ah. Well.

The world suddenly seemed a very boring place. I could feel the November greyness closing in on me. Nothing ever works well in November. So I opted for the decisiveness that I only ever genuinely feel on about the twelfth of July, the end of the summer term.

'Alastair,' I said. 'Forgive me, but you are being a bit tedious. No, in fact you are being *very* tedious. You have talked of nothing but yourself for the last hour. You have talked of your relations – and your lack of them, come to that. You have asked me about me and then talked of yourself again. You seem oblivious to this lovely place to which you have brought me.'

'I'm terribly sorry,' he said. 'I do find first meetings

hard, and when you didn't say anything at the beginning, I thought, well, I thought it was my go.'

'I see. But look, as we've been told in our pep talk, well, I have anyway, everyone finds first meetings difficult. But I would say, from my limited experience, that the best way is to ask the other person questions and then *listen* to the answers.'

'Oh right, yes, I see.'

And I suddenly thought how odd it was that this man could probably disentangle the complex legal language of some hideous divorce document but could not say the words 'what' or 'do' or 'you' or 'think' or 'of' in a relaxed fashion. Maybe, he didn't know (like bad teachers) how to ask the right question.

'You want a question. Well, right. Do you invest your, er-er, earnings or do you just keep some extra in your current account? I've always been interested in the way people manage their money.'

'I haven't.'

'Oh well, investing is the best option. My father was a fantastic investor. He once invested a hundred pounds in Scottish Widows, admittedly when they were doing well, and it doubled in a month.'

I put my hands over my ears. So much the right place and so much the wrong person in it. You would love it here, I thought. I felt sorry for Alastair; when one knows the mistake one has made, one does tend to make it again and again.

*

'I want to please you,' you said, just like Lawrence but not in the same patronising way. 'I want to give you all the pleasure you deserve.'

Oh, Jamie. I knew what you meant. You meant you wanted me to come, to hear me call out and move while that lovely swell and burst opened all over you. You prized those moments when I seemed close. 'Good, good,' you'd encourage, as if I had got my sums right. 'Good.' And in the first months, an instinctive move this way or that on my part would bring me on fast. But later, it was not like that and I knew that you worried. I knew that you thought it was because of you or because I didn't desire you.

Once, I pretended. To other women, to me with other men, lying about coming seems unimportant, but not so with us. We had always agreed to tell each other the truth, 'however hard'. But once I white-lied. Because it was almost an orgasm. The beginnings of one, *at least* two thirds of one.

I was sitting up on you, my T-shirt rucked up over my breasts. I love that position. I love seeing your body, relaxed, surrendered, except for your cock, which is inside me. I started to move on you, wishing I really knew what it felt like for you. I realise that in my head, the pictures are always of myself in activity. I cannot imagine therefore the pleasure you take in this passive position. But I know you like it. I can feel it now, me bending towards you, pinching your nipples in that way that makes you flinch, fingering the hair on your chest, looking down from time to time at the meeting point between us, where you are firmly inserted, the colour of my pubic hair against the slightly different colour of yours.

'Gorgeous,' you said. And it was. It was! Then slowly I felt that swelling inside, that slow swelling itch and I knew that I was about to arrive. But you called out, 'Yes, yes!' And you wanted it so much that I arrived it. It didn't arrive, I arrived it. I felt so awful afterwards, like a child who has cheated, used a calculator in an exam where the sums should be done on the paper. *Cheated*.

'No, not quite,' said Maud, when I was watching her teach. 'You're nearly there, but you've got the x in the wrong place.'

'But it feels right *there*.'

'Maths is not to do with feeling,' said Maud, with a smile on her face. 'It feels good when you have got the x in the right place, but you have to get it there correctly, you have to reason your way through. Like this . . .'

And she sat next to the girl ('nurturing', I wrote down in the column on my evaluation form titled *Rapport*) and started the sum from the beginning: $x + y = z - p = 1 = 3 + x$ and $y/2 = 2$. 'You see? Now put the one there. Now take the equals sign away and there you are, you have it, you have y. No, don't cross the z out, you can just forget about the z. Once you have the y, you can forget about the z.'

'Mixed', I wrote in the column headed *Discipline*. The rest of the class were playing hairdressers.

A few nights later, I dreamt of Tanya Wright. She was wearing one of Maud Scream's cardigans and was standing on a platform, addressing a group of shareholders. 'I see everyone personally,' she announced. 'I have attended one hundred orgasms, some of them simple affairs, some stupendous. But, I repeat, to put your mind at rest regarding my ability to match x and y, exactly *one hundred* orgasms. Tanya Wright gets it right.' Applause.

'Why do we keep having to start again?' said one Isobel Salter to Maud. 'I've done this calculation five times and it still comes to a hundred. I'm *bored*, Mrs Scream. I'm bored and it'll never come right, because if it isn't right the fifth time, I don't see how it'll ever be right.'

If I were an inspector and not just a friendly colleague popping in to watch, my hand would have been itching to scribble on my evaluation sheet. Instead, I let the sheet slip to the floor. All I could see was that Maud had a soft spot for this child. It was Maud's last year, she really didn't care about the rest of the class, but this girl, who seemed to have the same trouble as her with brushing her hair in the morning, and legs which looked as if they had been put on the wrong way round so that the left knee pointed towards the right and the right towards the left ('Even God gets his angles wrong, Mrs Scream, look at my legs,' she seemed to say, as she kicked at the maroon carpet with her three-inch rubber heels), this girl was Maud's special friend.

What happened next is an aberration of the kind that occurs only, as above, in that deadly month of November. I did something stupid. Instead of ringing Bright Lights to rid myself of Alastair Whatever-his-name-was, I rang him myself.

'Oh, Dorcas, yes, Dorcas.'

'Alastair,' I rabbited, deliberately forgetting your little rule book, as below, about supper engagements. 'Would you like to come for a bite one evening?' (That sounded silly, for a start.)

'Yes please, that would be very nice. I thought I'd rather cocked it up.'

'We both did,' I said. 'Next Saturday?'

'Just let me look at the old, er-er, diary.'

Help! Never mind about the old, er-er, diary, *he* sounded about ninety.

Which you never do. Never. Even when issuing rules, or snoring in bed.

'Now listen,' you said, before I left your flat for the last time. 'A few warnings. It'll be a list, but it's important.'

'Do I need to take notes?'

'Take *note*.'

Cold tone. You were hurting.

'It's important. And it's because I'm a man, and quite simply this is how men are.'

'Right.' I still despair at the jollity that pours out of me when I am at my most miserable.

'One: if you invite someone to dinner, they'll expect sex, even if the expectation is only at the back of their minds. Two: if a man rings you the day after you've met him, it means he's keen. Check to see that you really are. Three—'

'Stop! You're talking to me as if I am a teenager and also as if you genuinely do want me to kick around with all and sundry,' I said, hitching my khaki satchel over my shoulder.

'No, I'm not. Honestly not, Dorcas. But you do give off a sort of teenager feel. I can't quite think of the word for it.'

'Don't let me go then,' I wailed.

'We've had this conversation. And we know why we're doing what we're doing.'

I took your face between my hands, kissed you and walked to the door.

'Oh,' you added, 'and if there's a real emergency, please telephone me. Won't you?'

I said nothing, just walked out of your flat and into that horrible lift.

He arrived ten minutes early.

'Um, so sorry. But here I am.'

'You're welcome, Alastair,' I said, already regretting the invitation. I had been trying out the 'vulnerable people are better on second meetings' theory, indirectly inspired by Maud. Now I doubted the theory completely. Alastair had brought flowers and wine and was wearing a mustard-coloured waistcoat.

'I like that,' I said.

'Bit odd isn't it, but I rather like it too and there aren't many places one can celebrate it,' he confessed. Better. Better. Warming up, though I suppose the comment could have been taken as an insult.

'Can I help you with the cooking or are we having cold?'

Good. Very good. *Do* the cooking would be grand, though 'are we having cold' reminded me of my parents. How delicate the early stages of romance are. Every word is under scrutiny.

'Oh yes, I mean would you mind sorting out those roast potatoes? They seem to have gone wrong.'

'Apron?' he enquired coyly, and I threw him a flowery number, which he happily donned, then rolled up his sleeves. Quite nice arms and a sudden reduction in er-ers.

He sorted out the potatoes, suggested a quick way of making gravy and also of testing a joint of lamb (oh, lamb!) to see if it's ready without being blinded by spitting fat.

'Thanks so much,' I said. 'I'm rotten in the kitchen.'

'I think you're doing very well,' he said, and I felt like Isobel Salter with her back-to-front legs, being encouraged by Maud Scream: slightly irritated but pleased at the same time because I'd thought I was in charge and now he seemed to be.

Then he opened the wine. 'Cheers,' he jollied. 'Here's to the washing-up.'

Behind us a stack of filthy pans sat precariously in the sink. Why did that make me feel so relieved?

'Well,' said Maud at lunchtime, when half the children had been out of lessons, rehearsing the school play, '*I* had my class playing board games in maths. No point going on with pie charts with half of them not there.' She rescued a piece of tomato-covered spaghetti which was hanging down her chin; she always spoke with her mouth full, hence all the shirts she wore to school were lightly stained in exactly the same spot. 'No point pretending everything's fine, is it?' she went on, looking round the whole table. 'The school play wrecks teaching completely.'

Maud in fact loved school plays. She did the tickets, a business over which a pleasantly stubborn streak emerged. It worked a treat with bullish parents: 'Well, I'm afraid you just can't have that seat, Lord Holland, whatever your ticket says. The mayor's in it. All right? I'll give you this one. There you are. Yes, that way, up to the back row on the left. Restricted view. Never mind. There are worse things in life, are there not?'

Alastair had something of the same reassuring effect on me as he sorted out the kitchen: the sense, which I never had when alone, that all was well with the world and that 'that way' – spooning fat slowly, basting potatoes one by one – was the only way of doing it. Alone, with all the possible ways of performing an action, the world is a tiring place.

By seven forty-five, the washing-up was done, we were eating and all was well with the kitchen. We talked easily. No monologues, no lectures. A conversation. About nothing much, but definitely a conversation. I thought, You're a decent guy, I'm glad I invited you, after all.

Alastair clearly felt comfortable too. Because he stayed. He stayed for an hour after the meal was finished, drinking coffee. And then we went into the sitting room. Here, I made an incorrect calculation and sat on the sofa. I always sat there and forgot to be careful. And behold, there he was beside me, his arm trying to decide where to put itself. Eventually it opted for the back of the sofa, inches from my shoulders. I could feel it approaching.

'Do you want to watch a DVD?' I asked, jumping up.

'Yes, why not?' he said, undoing his waistcoat.

Forgetting what he had said about Rakhmaninov, I chose *Brief Encounter*, set it going and plonked myself on the beanbag. Alastair shifted about on the sofa, got comfortable and started watching.

'All right?' I asked.

'Oh yes, fine, thank you.'

'I know you've probably seen it but I thought you'd like the steam trains.'

'Oh yes, good.'

Silence. Twenty minutes passed. Clearly Alastair was bored while, even on a third viewing, I was transfixed. The funny clipped voices. And . . . the sadness of it.

'Look,' he said at one point. 'Look at the way that woman's pouring the tea.'

I hadn't noticed anything about the woman pouring the tea, was just watching the two struggling lovers.

A few minutes later, Alastair was asleep. Upset, I got up quietly and went to get some marking that I should have done the week before. Back to the beanbag. Rustle, rustle. I turned the volume down. I didn't want to see. Little snore. Then a hand moved towards my head and started stroking my hair.

Why wasn't it you? Why was it not you as you were those times I slept in your bed and you, so aware that even in your sleep you knew when I was dreaming something awful and needed the crook of your shoulder to rest in? How did you know? And why did you not mind me waking you so often to be comforted?

'What is it?'

'I dreamt you'd decided never to see me again.'

'Well, I'm here,' you said gently. 'And I'll never not see you again.'

And, still half asleep, you stroked my hair and held me to that warm body that did genuinely always seem to smell of lamb.

'I do not smell of lamb.'

'You do, you do. It's' – sniff – 'gorgeous.'

'Go to sleep,' you said, but with nothing of that self-preserving tone of the lover who doesn't want to be disturbed *any more*, thank you. For you, sleeping and loving slipped easily into each other.

When Alastair woke up, it was after midnight. The kitchen was tidy, we had eaten well and my marking was finished. I felt peaceful and a little wary at the same time.

'So sorry about the napping. It's a habit.'

'Don't worry,' I said airily, walking towards the door, wondering if it wasn't his fault rather than Diana's that their 'relations' had been limited. 'I did all my marking.'

'Good-good,' he said, and suddenly looked confused. I was now standing in front of the door, ready to open it for him. He buttoned his waistcoat, left his jacket on the sofa and came towards me.

Help!

No, no. Please, no. Yes, yes, said his face. Please, yes. And suddenly the full weight of him was against me.

'Wonderful evening. Lovely meal,' and his mouth moved towards mine, all wet and doggyish.

I thought of you standing in that very spot. How unreservedly I had kissed you there, and how many, many times. *And this wasn't you.* Same build, same slowish pace. But not you. *Not you.* I was suddenly so furious, so tired, so anguished that I bit Alastair's chin *really* hard.

'Gracious,' he said.

'Not gracious, not a bit gracious,' I cried out, 'but

108

you're the wrong person. I'm so very sorry. Your jacket. Please don't forget your jacket. Thank you so much for doing the washing-up. I'm so sorry, Alastair.'

'I rather liked having you in my lesson,' Maud said to me when we met in the photocopying room the next day.

'Did you? I wrote some not very nice comments on that stupid evaluation sheet. Weren't you cross about them?'

'Och, no,' said Maud. 'I'm used to it. Anyway, you're not the inspector after all.'

'I was pretending to be one,' I said, trying to cut a wodge of pink card with the guillotine.

'Oh, but you're no substitute for the inspector, Dorcas. I've got something quite different lined up for him. Or it might be a she, might it not? You're trying to cut too many pieces at once there, I think. That's why the card's coming out crooked.'

'Oh. Thanks.'

'Not a bit. Cutting things in the right way takes a wee bit of experience, Dorcas.' And she bumbled off cheerfully towards the dining room where the blackboard advertised beef stroganoff (i.e. stew). Beside it there was a picture of a butcher's knife.

English

The GCSE English syllabus is carved up into about eight chunks. I say about because each time I come to teach it, I have to check it again. So do all the members of the English department, particularly Pork, who has a bad memory for what the chunks are in the first place, which ones he has already done with his particular group and which are still to go. At the end of the two-year course, he habitually honks, 'You should have told me.' 'You should have read the syllabus,' I honk back. 'I even sent off for your own special copy, which I labelled with your name as you had lost yours.' (Inspector Hereford notes down, *management style: worse than poor.*)

In any case, one of the much-loved units of work at GCSE level is autobiographical writing. This year, I teach an unusually charming group of lower-set girls. So, instead of setting the usual 'My Most Favourite Person in the World' (characterisation) or 'The Prettiest Place in Sussex' (setting) or 'My Most Embarrassing Moment' (plot), I said, 'Right, let's get to the heart of what your minds are busy with. "My First Boyfriend". In by next Monday, which gives you time to find a boy if you haven't one already. Bullet points to help your thinking as follows. Bullet: Where you met. Bullet: First impressions. You know, was he spotty but turned out to be compassionate or have a nice mouth or whatever? Bullet: Your first argument, if you got that far.' ('Slow down, slow down, Miss Trevelyan.') 'Bullet: How it ended, if it did. Bullet the fifth: What your parents thought of him. Right? Good.'

Shrieks followed. They always do when you say 'good' like that.

'I've only had one boyfriend.'

'Fine. Him then.'

'I don't have one.'

'I've already covered that eventuality.'

'I don't like boys.'

'Well, "My First Girlfriend" then.'

Hands rushed to mouths.

'Well, statistically there's likely to be one lesbian amongst us.'

'It might be you,' came a whoop.

'It might indeed, but in fact I have . . .'

'Yes, yes?'

'I have a male friend.'

'You write about him, then,' shouldered in a giant of a girl called Polly. 'We'll only do ours if you do yours.'

'All right,' I said, not wanting a tricky encounter with

the giant. 'I'd be only too happy. In by Monday,' I repeated, aware of the justified indictment that English teachers set tasks related exclusively to their own pre-occupations.

The next day, in the middle of the one thousandth chapter of *Wuthering Heights*, I threw in, 'By the way, when you do your boyfriend pieces – *in on Monday* – please do them as if addressing a magazine. You know the sort of thing. "Dear Mariella, I have just reached the end of a disastrous relationship . . ."'

'No, no, that's *boring*. We just want to write it as it is.'

Ah, well.

'Well, actually, so do I,' I said. 'So I suppose that's all right then. On we go.'

(*Head of English at St Edmund's College: empathetic but too pliable*. Chief Inspector Hampshire.)

Not My First Boyfriend

'Do you know those days when you wake up feeling something important is going to happen?' my account began, to a room of attentive listeners. 'Well, the day I met the Professor was not a day like that. I felt instead a reluctance to get up at all. I would have rather lain in bed and read some more of Tolstoy, but I had to go to London to buy some resources to support the teaching of this dismal English Language course you all love so much. (Note the use of sarcasm.)

'I won't go into the tedious nature of the journey, the stink of the Underground and the cold wind that always makes me feel a mess. (Note the ironic use of ellipsis here.) I will simply tell you that I arrived at Hatchards at eleven o'clock, wearing jeans and an enormous jumper (I hate coats) such as you might wear on a Scottish island. (Note the sudden broadening of the narrative.)

'Can't you stop interrupting and just read the story, Miss Trevelyan!' snapped the giant, in a state of genuine agitation.

'How will you learn about writing if I do that?'

'Oh, that doesn't matter.'

'All right.' (Inspector Hertford (BA Oxon): *Leniency again*.)

'Anyway, I went straight to the English Language section where there was the usual boring collection of books on how to write for different audiences, how to write articles, how to analyse words, phrases, even punctuation and I thought, yes, yes, I *know*. But last year, our results in Language were down and one of my colleagues who shall remain nameless to you, and who is very keen on "banks of resources" implored me to make this little trip. So here I was. It took me fifteen minutes to make my choice: two slim volumes containing clearly explained units of work, which I could impose upon you on those days when I am more in the mood for filing my nails (joking, girls) or simply not up to the constant stream of words that you, who cannot read more than five hundred words of pre-twentieth-century prose without needing to get out your hairbrushes, mirrors and make-up in order to remind yourselves of the fact that you are all that is best in the modern girl, demand of me as mere background accompaniment. (There are a lot of techniques used here but I won't go into them.)'

'Good.'

'*In any case*, I arrived at the till with my tomes. (Alliteration for effect.) There was no queue and, feeling, for some reason, embarrassed, I moaned to the till girl about my dull purchase and how I wished I could have bought the new biography of Coleridge instead.

'"Yes, it's very good," I heard a voice behind me. I turned round, while the till girl, who couldn't care a jot about my peevish state, got on with my Visa card. And there was a tall man with a hardback—'

'Who had a hard back?'

'Oh, do listen,' I said. 'Not a hard back, a hardback. A book. Book! Thing you read, or don't, sadly. He had a hardback in his hand. Actually, he was buying about three or four.'

'Oh.'

'If I described this man to you, young, critical and limited as you are, you would say that he sounds like your father. Suffice it to say that you would be lucky to have a relation of any kind with such a face; a face that one knows instantly one can trust. A seriousness too which I liked. And this wonderfully thick-set neck. (Don't make those faces. It was nice.)

'"I do sympathise," he said as I harrumphed at the extortionate sum of money for which I was to sign. "Not much fun forking out for that sort of thing."

'"Your books look inviting," I said.

'"Yes, I'm quite pleased," he remarked. "I've been wanting to read the Chekhov for years and the Ted Hughes on Shakespeare."'

At the mention of Shakespeare, my listeners sank into a gloom.

'I shall go *on*,' I said crossly. 'In any case, seeing my stunning face turned to his in the sudden morning sunlight, he dropped all his books on the floor, took me in his arms and kissed me in front of three other customers, the till girl, London walking past outside and of course all the assembled heritage of great English writers. That kiss . . . Oh, so sorry girls, that's as far as I've got. Your turn.'

'Did he really kiss you? You're mucking us about.'

'No, I'm not. It's absolutely true,' I said, remembering later kisses. 'But, as I say, no more from me, since you're such an unappreciative audience. Your go. Sky?'

'I'm not reading aloud.'

'Right, you can read Sally's.'

'No way,' said Sally.

'All right.' (Too pliant, too pliant.) 'Well does *anyone* want to read theirs?'

A surprising number of hands went up.

*

'Myfirstboyfriendwasfour—'

'Slow down, Sam.'

'My First Boyfriend Was Four And I Was Three. We met at nursery school. We used to fight a lot over a lastic porry—'

Roars.

'Don't worry, I do that all the time. It's called a Spoonerism.'

'Why?'

'I don't know. I think there was a Mr Spooner who did it a lot.'

'Oooh.'

'You know what I mean. Don't be silly. On you go, Samantha.'

'A *plastic lorry* that we both wanted to ride. I usually won, but one day, I was just lifting myself into the driving seat, my dress all spread around me like an umbrella . . . I can't spell that word.'

'Never mind, it's a tough one, I agree. Go on.' (Inspector Hereford: *Too much pacing going on for authoritative atmosphere to be created. Big weakness. Also no evidence that teacher herself knows how to spell umbrella.*)

'When Peter came up, knelt down and butted his head into the side of the lorry and it toppled over. It was like a real road accident. I was stuck in the lorry, my torso on the passenger seat and my head squashed between the floor and the side of the lorry. Peter stood in shock for a minute – he hadn't meant to hurt me, I don't think – and then he started doing ambulance noises and whirling his arms in the air. He came round to where my head was and kicked the side of the lorry so that it lay empty and I was on the floor with my dress over my face. Gently, he stroked me. Then Mrs Rosewood came up to ask if I was all right.

'"Want a plaster." I said. She got nasty then and said I shouldn't have been playing with the lorries, I should have been reading on a beanbag.

'About a week later, when we were having a special tea because it was that hot cross bun day thing, Peter kissed me. He had a mouthful though, so it wasn't great. Then he stroked me again. It didn't feel rude at the time, it felt nice. I invited him to my birthday party for the next two years and he brought me great presents. He also showed me his male organ once, under the table. Now he goes to St Gregory's and he's a real thug. I'm glad I had my "affair" with him when I did. That's it.'

'That was really good,' everyone agreed.

'Yes, it was,' I said pompously. 'Very good umbrella image too. Not unlike the sex scene in L. P. Hartley's *The Go-Between*. And a good structure. Nice ending. Language a touch colloquial but it's only a draft. Next? Gemma. Good.'

'Right. I got snogged—'

'Introduction?' I asked calmly.

'We didn't introduce ourselves.' I let it pass. 'I got snogged at this party by this bloke who was shorter than

117

me. I had to bend down so he could reach me, but I was wearing these mega heels—'

The bell rang.

'Let's miss music, Miss Trevelyan. Ple-e-ease. He won't notice. He's furious with us anyway.'

'Well, he will miss you then, won't he? Anyway, much as I would like to hear more about Gemma's experience I have another class to teach—'

'Excuse me Miss Trevelyan, but you're making us late,' said Charlotte, a serious and bright member of the class.

'Exactly,' I smiled, liking her high-minded impertinence. 'You're right. So off you go. See you tomorrow.'

They didn't hear my little farewell, which made me feel vulnerable, a trick at which they are unconsciously adept. Added to which, I did not in fact have another class to teach until the afternoon.

Sometimes, in moments of weakness during the school day, I disappear without telling anyone (not even you, Jamie). Just walk straight to my car, drive into East Grinstead and have a cup of tea or at worst buy myself a present – nothing as expensive as the green shoes, which still haven't arrived incidentally, but a notebook, at least, or a box of lush pens.

Maybe because I had made the high-minded Charlotte so late that she was running off shoulders at a slant under her load of books, I too began an awkward sprint in my high-heeled boots.

But where was my car? I scarpered about a bit, dropped my umbrella, left it where it was, deciding to have done once and for all with this tiresome accessory. I finally found the car parked in front of the new science block. I slung my bags into the boot and drove off. Today, it would be a present, I decided: a blast through the car wash. Maybe that would brighten me up ready for an afternoon of George Herbert, collected poems of.

The car felt a little chilly so I messed about with the heating, turned on the radio for the sound of a voice other than my own and put my foot down. There followed a big blast of cold air. I swivelled round, stretching quickly into the back seat to pick up one of my many woollen garments (scarves, ponchos, wraps) designed to protect me from the metallic texture of the world and did a balletic swerve that nobody saw because the road was empty.

But I saw. And, in the end, that is the worst – seeing oneself – especially as it wasn't just the swerve I caught myself for but also the boot, which I noticed was wide open and gently flapping. I giggled out loud, which is a quick way of weeping, pulled over, climbed out fast (no seatbelt either) and banged the boot closed. I was shaking and badly in need of one of those restorative phone calls with you, in which the required chiding is administered and then a verbal kiss. But there was no you and so instead it had to be the car wash.

On arrival, I switched off the radio and, being extra angry, asked the little, young, Indian owner for the most expensive combination of wax, polish, brush and scrub.

'I haven't seen you for a while,' he said, also remembering that I was a teacher – 'you should teach me English one day' – that I had recently had my brakes mended, that I had once been to Goa and today, as he took my money, he said, 'Why have you not been back to Goa, madam?'

'Too busy,' I said, referring both to Goa and his slow shenanigans with the jet-washing of my wheels.

'You can go forward now,' he said, beckoning me towards the *Wait until the light is green* notice. I watched the big blue brushes swathing foam all over a black car in front of me. Then I saw the white foam dribble to an unexpected stop and the Indian, plastic bags on his feet, rush towards the black car.

What's going on? I gestured.

He took no notice, disappearing into the machine then frantically waving at me, 'Back, back!' The machine had broken. The driver in front revved up, turned round to navigate a sharp retreat and lo, there was the face of the lovely Lawrence, he of the tie-pin eyes, his Porsche moving straight towards me until, after some fiddling about, we were parked adjacent to each other.

The Indian ran about back and forth from his little office to the machine and then came over to Lawrence, clearly urging him to have another go, 'Free of charge, it is all mended now, sir'. But no second goes for Lawrence. That most charming of men with the sensitive cock got out of his car and pointed furiously to his left wing mirror, which had been flattened like a bent ear. I lowered my window to listen to what he had to say.

'I'll be back with the bill for this,' he announced, pointing his forefinger at the Indian's nose.

The Indian told him gently, 'Sir, there is a notice over there which informs customers that management takes no responsibility for any vehicles.'

'I see,' said Lawrence. 'So let's just talk that through, shall we? I come in and your machine breaks down just as I am moving towards that bar over there which lowers and stops an inch or so away from the windscreen' (acting it out with his hands). 'I repeat, your machine breaks and the bar crashes down on to the windscreen which smashes and glass goes into my left eye.'

Here, Lawrence closed his eye with a malice so dramatically different from the wink he had given me in the pub that I put my hand to my throat and gasped.

'And you say that you do *nothing* about that?' Pointing to his left eye, '*Nothing?*'

'Is your eye hurt?' asked the Indian.

'It was just an example.'

'Well, as I say, sir, the notice informs customers that management takes—'

'So my broken wing mirror?'

'No responsibility. I'm so sorry, sir but I do know a man who—'

'No thanks,' said Lawrence and got heavily back into his car, slamming his door so close to the Indian's hand that I expected him to jump backwards. He then drove away in a swerve nearly as manic as my own.

Did he see me? I don't know, but I certainly saw him and he was a man I did not like.

'Poor you,' I said, really addressing myself. 'Is your hand all right? Is the machine really mended?'

'Definitely, madam, it was a power failure only. All OK for you now.' And he waved me towards the revolving brushes.

Inside the blueness, with the water pouring down my car, I had a proper cry. I was tired and upset and, once cleansed, on the outside at least, drove at a very fast lick back to the sanctuary of school.

And back to the recounting of my story to the giant and her friend Phoebe, who had 'a free period now, we promise, so ple-e-ease go on, but not too slowly because we've got hockey and, Miss Trevelyan, sorry, but your professor man sounds so *boring*.' I was still describing our first meeting.

'People, things, life are not what they seem,' I said emphatically. 'You need to know that. Besides, it's a truth central to the study of English literature.'

'Come *on*!' The giant hit her hand against the desk. 'Ow!'

'There, you see? You thought that would make you feel better but it hurt. Anyway, to continue. We're in London in the bookshop, remember?'

They settled themselves on the bourgeois footstools,

bought from junk shops, which I keep by the radiator for the purposes of proper talks.

.'You're obviously a keen reader,' I said to the Professor, painfully aware of how boring this sounded.

'Oh yes,' he enthused. 'I couldn't exist without. What about you? Do you like reading?'

'Yes, very much. But as a teacher, one tends to have to read texts over and over, which helps one to understand style, but, well, there are too many unread books.'

'Oh, of course, but that's the same for all of us,' he said, settling his load into an expensive-looking carrier bag. By this time, we had started walking towards the bestsellers display near the front of the shop.

'I wish I could write one of those,' I pined, stroking the cover of a paperback with a picture of a red-haired naked woman on it.

'Oh, you mustn't be beguiled by all of that. Most of it's modernist claptrap,' he said, looking at his watch. 'In any case, what are you doing now? Now, this minute?'

'I'm going home.'

'Which is?'

'East Grinstead.'

'Why don't we have coffee?'

I remember that first conversation vividly. It was conducted exactly as most of our conversations have been since: he talking, then me. We are both good listeners and neither of us likes to be interrupted. He told me about his son Joshua, who was at university in London reading history, told me that he himself was a professor of English at Queen Mary, and that he had a flat high up on Parliament Hill, with a wonderful view of London. 'Josh has his own digs,' he said, 'so I have the solitude I need to do my writing.' (He did not, at that point, mention his wife, just as I will not mention her to the girls.)

'Writing?'

'I used to write biographies, but recently, like many ageing arties, I've been having a bash at fulfilling my ambition to write a decent play. Hence,' he said, patting his bag of books, 'Chekhov's letters.'

I had two utterly clear thoughts as I sat watching him. First, I thought how lucky Joshua was to have him as a father. And then I thought how much I would like to be his wife.

'Ohhh,' moaned the giant. 'Why do we have to have all that stuff about *books* and coffee? Did you go to bed with him?'

'Look,' I said crossly, 'you can't just jump in—'

'No, not jump in, but you could get into bed nice and slowly, Miss Trevelyan.'

'You can't just jump in *when writing about something important*. As I told Gemma, to have "snogging", as you call it, in the very first paragraph is vulgar.'

'Well, you said to jump in when we wrote about *Wuthering Heights*.'

'Yes, that's because I set you an essay titled, "How far can we sympathise with Heathcliff?" And half of you started with: "I am going to talk" – wrong for a start as you're writing – "about how I do sympathise with Heathcliff and then I am going to talk about how I don't sympathise with Heathcliff and then I am going to put them together and see which is the longest." Which sounds as if you are doing carpentry. But, when writing fiction—'

'You said it was non-fiction.'

'When writing *creatively* then, you do not get ticked for good points, it's the overall effect of the piece. Anyway, didn't you say you had hockey? We'll hear an account from someone else in the next lesson since you're so clearly unworthy of hearing more of mine. Off you go.'

The Toothpaste Touch, 28 November, by Harriet Jones

'My first boyfriend was my cousin Nathan. I know people say romantic liaisons with cousins is trouble, but we never had sex and so I haven't given birth to a thermalide or whatever those people are called. Nathan and I had known each other since birthhood, but it was three summers ago when our families were on holiday that our relationship changed. We were in a cottage in Devon. Ten of us all squashed in. Though it was raining, we still all, I mean, we all still went surfing and swimming. And when we came back, we fought to get the first hot bath as we were so cold.

'One day, it had been really freezing and we went into

the bathroom in twos to hurry things up. We were only eleven so Mum pushed Nathan and me in together. I don't remember feeling at all shy. He was like a brother. Well, at least he was until he got undressed that day.'

Shrieks.

'*Well*, at least he was, until he got undressed. We were both shivering like anything and our wet bathers sat on the floor while we splashed about in the water. He had a lovely smooth body. I looked at him and I thought, I love you. You're like my brother, you're my best friend, I love you. That night, we played loads of—'

'Don't write loads of.'

'That night, then, we played *many* paper games and *many* card games and we also ate *many* chips. Everyone seemed particularly happy. Before bed, Nathan and I met again in the bathroom to brush our *many* teeth.'

'Don't be like that.'

'Our two heads touched—'

'Did you each have two heads?' asked the giant calmly.

I could see tears gathering. 'Stop it. Go on, Harriet, it's excellent.'

'As-as-as we bent over the basin, I heard this clunk. Nathan had dropped his toothbrush into the basin and was holding me around the waist. By this time, Nathan was wearing pyjama bottoms and I was in a T-shirt. Then-then-then he kissed my toothpasty mouth, while holding my bare back under my T-shirt.'

'Oooh.'

'STOP IT!'

I am a gentle teacher on the whole but ridicule of a child is not something I tolerate. 'Go on, Harriet,' I said in a voice that didn't sound like mine.

'That-that-that summer, we kissed every day and on the last day of the holiday—'

'You had sex,' came a cry from the back of the classroom.'

'*On the last day* of the *many* days of our holiday, when the sun came out for the first time, we sat on the beach together and agreed that we would allow each other four other serious relationships with other people, just for the experience, but then we'd get married. Unfortunately, I haven't had even one relationship yet, so at this rate I have worked out that I won't marry Nathan until I am at least thirty. But I am willing to wait. The end.'

This piece received a standing ovation. In some way, it upset me, because it both reminded me of our decision to *wait*, and it also recalled childhood holidays when I too had experienced the first exciting beginnings of love, when there was time to make mistakes and there were adults who would come to the rescue if things became difficult, whereas now, in this ghastly process of encountering men jaded by past failures, there is no one to tell but you.

When the bell went, I let them go, without setting more homework.

Once more, the giant and Phoebe lolled about, not wanting to go.

'Miss Trevelyan,' Phoebe said shyly, with that wiggle of her puppy-fat torso which always makes me want to hug her, 'we know we were a bit rude yesterday, but we'd, well, I'd like to hear the rest of your story about the bookshop man.'

'I haven't written any more.'

'Go on with it, then,' ordered the giant. 'Then we can meet at lunchtime and have a packed lunch and do a critique of it. On Friday. Can we do it on Friday?'

'Yes, yes, but off you go now.' (*Head of English not only encourages confessional writing of a kind capable of embarrassing a vulnerable student, but also unburdens herself in their presence.* Inspector Hertford.)

Yes, but I love them, I defended in my head. I love and I know them, which takes us a long way, I can tell you.

That night, I continued writing.

'I'll tell you about Victoria,' said Jamie. This statement should have hurt, but behind the bluntness was an entreaty, which softened me. 'She's five years younger than I am. She works near London Bridge. A solicitor. She got a top first in English at Cambridge and when we married and had Joshua, she didn't want to work. But ten years ago, she took a law degree and now, as I say, she's a solicitor.'

'That's brilliant,' I said, strongly aware that, behind his pride, there was something wrong, something odd or forced or unhappy about her. Or was there something wrong with me? Or even with you? (I mean him.)

Why did you (I mean he) paint her in such a daunting way?

'She has a flat in the Barbican. We prefer living apart during the week. She comes back to our flat in Parliament Hill on a Friday.'

Two flats in London seemed strange to me, but I confess to quite liking strangeness.

'And what about you?' enquired the professor ('Call me Jamie').

'Well,' I began, 'I used to live in a caravan in West Sussex, with no running water. But last year my caravan was washed away by the floods and now I live in a hand-made wigwam in the woods down the road.'

He sat back and smiled a smile that could carry every ounce of my silliness and also of my sadness.

'Oh, come on,' he said softly.

'Well, OK.' And off I went with much more of my story than I had meant to tell. There was something about his face that made me want to tell, to pour into him all my intensity, all my upsets and hurts, as well as some of my achievements, which he always made one feel were more considerable than they were.

'And men?' he asked. 'Do you have a—'

'Not at the moment. I'm hesitant. Spiritual confusions.'

'I understand. I was going to go into the church myself at one time, but like old Coleridge, I couldn't find my niche.'

'I found mine too easily,' I said.

'Well, you're very lucky.'

I suddenly felt unlucky, as if I had missed out on years of loving this man. I wondered what Jamie had looked like when he was twenty. I had an idea he had become more handsome with age.

'You're a thinker. That's good,' he went on, confidently slurping his coffee. This man has been to lots of restaurants, I thought. He uses toothpicks and things after four-course dinners, and discusses book contracts. And then I felt happy.

As we were leaving, he took a small notepad from his inside pocket and wrote down his address.

'Would you, er, would you write to me?' he asked quietly. And I felt I had been catapulted back to a safer, better century.

'I'd like that,' I said, feeling very nervy. 'Will you write back?'

'Of course. Write and tell me about your reading, write about anything.'

'Thank you so much.'

We shook hands outside the restaurant. He had big hands. I had watched them as they rested flat on the table. Strong, practical hands that could navigate their way around the entire stretch of one of England's most complex motorways. I felt him trying out my fingers, holding them gently and then deciding to enfold them.

'I'm glad we met.'

'Yes,' I said, and walked away with stupid tears in my eyes. He had a wife, a son, a life.

'I thought what you wrote was good,' said Phoebe on Friday, when we were sitting on the footstools eating packed lunches. 'Why didn't you go on?'

'No time. I know how you feel about homework deadlines now. It's tough fitting everything in.'

'Exactly,' said the giant. 'So, my piece will be in on Wednesday at the earliest.'

'I see,' I said wryly.

'Anyway, Miss Trevelyan, I've got an idea. Why don't you just *tell* us what happened next?'

'Please would you?' added Phoebe. I looked sheepish. 'We don't have any experience. We want to know. And we won't judge.'

'And it will go quicker too,' added the giant. 'Maybe the whole class could skip doing any writing and all just say our pieces out loud. You know, an oral. On *Wednesday*.'

I knew that what I was about to do, like so much I have done in my life, was both entirely wrong and absolutely right. There was quite simply no other teacher I knew who would indulge this conversation, though I suppose I could justify it under the differentiation policy.

Besides, I knew just how much it would have meant to me as a fifteen-year-old, how much I would have loved to have been told such a story.

'Go on, go on,' urged the giant.

'It will take more than twenty minutes.'

'Well, start, start.'

'I have never been one for etiquette.'

'What's that?'

'You know, wearing the right thing for the right occasion and all that sort of thing.'

'No,' they chorused, 'we noticed.'

'So, instead of leaving a respectable gap of at least four days, I wrote to the Professor the next day. And it wasn't a short note either. It was a three-page typed letter all about what I was reading, how I was feeling a bit lost for direction, how I quite liked Sussex but didn't want to live here for ever. He wrote back by return of post. And I'll tell you girls, when that envelope thudded through the letter box on to my dark green mat, my heart did the same. I felt as if it was the first time it had ever beaten in my life.

'In his letter, the Professor referred to nothing I had said about myself, but wrote an entire commentary on a poem by John Donne, which he had been re-reading. I had told him over coffee that I was teaching the Metaphysicals that year and I sometimes found it hard not to make it too dry. Then, in the last paragraph, he wrote, "I would very much like to meet you again. I thought you a charming and unusual person." Something like that. And I knew then that he was someone who would not answer one's questions immediately, but would store them up for the right moment.

Phoebe and the giant starting jigging up and down on their footstools. 'So? When? Where? Did he kiss you? Really, this time?'

'Stop it,' I snapped. 'We wrote to each other a few more times before we met. I think he was trying out all sides of his personality on me first: the serious academic side; the silly amusing side; the sad side.'

I am sure they would have liked to read your letters, but that is taking 'differentiation' too far. And as for telling them at all, I wonder what you would think, Jamie. Just understand that, somehow, these two children seemed, in their innocence, to be my safest confidantes.

'Then what? Then what?' they hurried me again.

'Well . . . Then he had to go abroad for three weeks. But for some reason – perhaps we didn't want to break the still-fragile and sparkling connection that was being spun between us – we spoke on the phone every day. Then . . . then, he came to stay. All details omitted. Let's just say all went well.'

At that point, my saintly, as in mistake-free, colleague Lucy appeared in the classroom, her pale-blue trouser suit so calming.

'Dorcas,' said she, 'there's an Accelerated Learning meeting. It starts in two minutes.' (I won't bore you with an explanation of what this means.)

'Sure not in seven seconds?' I whinged.

'Oh, and I don't know if you noticed, but there's a Health and Safety meeting after school as well,' she added. 'By the way, did you hear on the radio that children have to wear safety masks when they play conkers now?'

'Oh, I heard that,' said the giant. 'My mum said conkers have been banned completely in schools because of nut allergies.'

I started giggling and unceremoniously shoved the girls out of the room.

We did not make an appointment for the next episode. It would arrive in its own time, as formal meetings never do; formal meetings always occur at entirely the wrong time, as if God arranges them as a form of tedious protection against intimacy. For, emerging from any St Edmund's meeting, I always feel as if someone has sharply pulled up my socks, brushed my hair and told me to mind my language. This meeting was no different. Indeed, the main item on the agenda was language. *Affirmative* language.

'This is not just for the inspection. Appropriate language use is, as we know, a part of school policy – see the pink section 2B, part 1, in the school handbook,' said Our Headmistress. 'And I would like the Accelerated Learning trainers to include a unit on this in their course. Everyone all right with that? Good. And by the way, I have heard from some staff that the way years ten and eleven answer questions in class shows a lack of respect. They're getting sloppy.'

She's right, I thought, but I also knew that the moderate success of my lessons was dependent on a sharp repartee that would not have worked if curbed by good manners.

*

That weekend, I marked the entire batch of 'My First Boyfriend' pieces. I gave them all at least grade B, because they were bloody brave, and I gave a couple of them an A, because they were absolutely brave. Subjective marking systems always work best, reduce the labour and are generally adequate. Compare this comment of mine, for example, with that used for the same grade by the compilers of the syllabus.

Me: *I loved this. It made me laugh. It was also poignant and the dialogue was plausible. I thought William was as much of a prat as you do, but weren't you a bit harsh on him in the last paragraph? The words you used there just tilted what was a funny piece over into being more cruel than I think you meant it to be. You're great at structure. I envy you that! Grade A.*

Exam syllabus: *Grade A work is characterised by strong form, sophisticated syntax and an appropriate use of language. The candidate will show themselves to be proficient at handling the balance between dialogue and description and have a firm hold on the pace of the writing. The work will be neatly presented, each page joined to the next with a green treasury tag and slipped neatly into a transparent folder for safekeeping.*

I made the treasury tag bit up, naturally. But you get the idea.

I have always struggled with clashes of language. I have never been entirely clear about informal and formal in any context and I envy children because largely they are forgiven and loved for their indiscretions. Perhaps, in some unconscious way, I was jealous of Phoebe and the giant and wanted to get them into trouble, because when they badgered me in the corridor about episode three of 'The Professor', I suggested we all miss the Christmas bazaar, which is held in the gym. It is a chronic event. Like entering hell for the afternoon and, although it answered – along with the sponsored walk, the sponsored swim, the famine lunches, the donate-a-pound-to-wear-your-own-clothes day (which I never paid for on principle as I would not wear anyone else's clothes in the first place, except yours sometimes, your big denim shirts that smell of an aftershave whose name I don't know but which I do know I like, and of lamb of course) – all of Mr Hampshire's questions about the school's contributions to charity, it seemed to me a deeply uncharitable event, designed to damage the ears and bring on a migraine. Much better to dress up warm and huddle in the sunken garden by the swimming pool with cups of tea stolen from the staff room and educate Phoebe and the giant in the perils of love.

They were thrilled at the prospect, bringing with them the next day not only coats but blankets while the giant, not one for sitting on the ground, brought three deckchairs, which she had told her mother were needed for the bazaar.

'Bloody hell,' said the giant, struggling, as does the rest of humanity, with the erection of the deckchairs.

'That's not right . . .'

'Nor's that.'

'We'll have to use them as groundsheets if you deal with them like that.'

Once we had sorted ourselves out and were firmly seated in a row, under blankets, tea in hands, Phoebe urged, 'So, Miss Trevelyan, what happened next?'

'Well, the next thing was a weekend at Jamie's flat.' This was a lie, but it was the part that I wanted to talk about. Questions rippled out into the Christmas air.

'No, wait, wait. I'll tell you about it, then you can ask afterwards. It was a tasteful flat. Big rooms, masses of books, low coffee tables, white bedlinen, two power showers, widescreen TV and, how else can I describe it? Not lush, but *right*. Everything worked properly. I think I felt, when I entered that flat, that it was the first time I had really entered the adult world, a place, it seems to me, where you have a right to expect certain standards.'

Sniggers from the giant.

'It was during this weekend too that I began to see on how many different levels the Professor lived. He always appeared relaxed, but I could see that, in fact, I had never seen him truly relaxed. Confident yes, but not relaxed. A person can only be themselves when they are on their own, he had once told me. Why did I feel hurt by this even though I could see the truth of it?'

Phoebe looked down into her tea and I thought I noticed her slip a little lower in her deckchair.

'Our love has been, or it was anyway, a journey.'

'Oh come on, Miss Trevelyan,' sighed the giant. 'Hurry up with the story.'

'Our love,' I continued, my face poking proudly out over the top of the blanket, 'was a journey. Each time we met, we moved another step. These forward movements were largely manifested in our sexual activity. There, satisfied? Now, don't blush. Really, don't. When you are an open person like me, it is easy to speak, to be *verbally* honest. But sometimes it is only when the speaking is done physically that you can really tell what you are saying to each other. Your body draws back from some things and tells you, you have not reached that place yet.'

(You see, Inspector Halifax, sex education is best done on a one to one basis. Banish all those sessions with condoms on bananas.)

'That weekend was a delight. The Professor is not one of those men – and, girls, you will meet them in their dozens – for whom sex is a quick race to the end. He likes to go slowly, because he knows that as soon as he has finished, he'll want to write the next act of his play or rail at a politician on television. It is a fact of biology to which he owns up and which he himself doesn't like. In fact, the more we stroke and hold each other, the more we simply touch, the better the sex is afterwards. I think everyone wishes for, even requires, that kind of touch.'

'Requires!' sneered the giant.

'Yes, requires. So don't worry too much. Some men, a very few I would think, aren't the boom-boom-and-it's-over types. They are ready to wait.'

Phoebe had that baby-with-wind look again. Something needed to come out.

'But, Miss Trevelyan,' she said. 'He did love you, didn't he? He wasn't just, you know . . .'

'Using me, you mean?'

'Yes,' said Phoebe.

'Well, you know I have come to think –' (here the giant yawned) – 'I have come to think that love is about using each other, but it is done with permission.'

'I s'pose,' said Phoebe. But something was troubling her.

'Phoebe, it wasn't all sex. We sat and talked about everything we'd ever done and cared about. I told him about my parents and my childhood. I told him about my body, its failings and strengths. We talked about the merits and deceptions involved in the dyeing of hair, the wearing of make-up, the dealing with constipation.'

'Eeew!'

'No, I mean it. There were no taboos, which, for me, who was brought up in a family where intimate conversations were excruciating, was a relief. Such a relief.'

'And what did he tell *you*?' asked the giant, as bad as Phoebe on the judgement front.

'Again, everything he could remember. His first girlfriend, the students he had dallied with during his lecturing days, his innate pessimism, his . . .' And I stopped there. We sat back in our deckchairs under our rugs like the three witches.

'Do you like Mrs Block?' asked the giant suddenly.

'Right, time to go,' I said, recognising that this pleasant little scene was moving fast towards a bad end. 'I think you'd better go to the gym now and chuck a few balls.'

'I'll aim them at Mrs Block,' said the giant, who had been given two detentions, one for breaking a percussion instrument and the other for locking the diminutive junior music master in a book cupboard.

'As you wish,' I replied, leaving her to fold the deckchairs while I dealt with the tea cups.

'I've been chucked out of the choir,' said Phoebe as I was leaving.

'Oh, Phoebe, why?'

'For getting the harmonies wrong. They said the mayor's concert would be spoilt if I was in it.' The giant sniggered in a kindly sort of way.

It's hard to forget the occasion when you disturbed our harmony. Perhaps because it came too soon. Whatever the reason, I could not describe it to the giant and particularly not to Phoebe, who was a child still in need of the illusion that all adults are good.

You knew it was a risk, the sort of risk an artist takes and, once it is set in motion, knows he has to see through. 'I want you to meet my wife and son,' you said.

'*What?*'

'I know . . . I know. But . . .'

You turned to me, looked right at me and said, 'The thing is that when someone is important, you want them to know you fully, to see you in different situations. It's a struggle. Victoria. Not Joshua. Joshua's fine.'

'Does he know?'

'No. But Victoria, she's hard, in all senses of the word. I need you to see her, to know what she's like, so that you can fully understand the situation. It would help you to know me better. I know it's a lot to ask but I'd organise it so there were other people there. We'll make it a sort of drinks party. Look at me, Dorcas. Don't cry. Listen. If you were just a passing fancy, I wouldn't be asking you this. Would you? Please?'

'OK,' I said, 'but how will you explain it in practical terms? Who will you say I am?'

'Don't worry about that. I'll think of something, and if there are other people there it will be fine.'

Why did I not refuse? Why did I not say to you: Jamie, I can't, I won't, it would be too difficult.

I remember, as I went into my kitchen after that conversation, feeling very much not an adult. I thought of women I knew of my own age, who would have considered this request outrageous. But you were different. I was different. We were each emotionally strange, I think; both very young and very old at the same time, though you could play at being grown up much more successfully than me. Besides, I wanted to please you.

And also, I like things that are hard because they force you to grow up.

'Where have you two been?' I heard Our Headmistress asking Phoebe and the giant, while I toyed with a fairy cake from a Year Seven stall.

'We went for a walk.'

'You're selfish,' she boomed. (Why do teachers so often think volume and authority are synonymous?) 'And immature. This event, frivolous as it might seem, is not about *you*, it's about *you* raising money for *other people*. Charity. Giving. Maturity is about thinking about other people, not about yourselves all the time. That is what maturity is.'

(Disagree, I thought, struggling, a few stalls away, with a blob of green icing.)

'And you, by going for a walk, were doing the opposite. Thinking *only* of yourselves.'

'We weren't on our own,' blurted Phoebe (never a good liar).

'Sorry,' said the giant, suddenly. She stood solid as a policeman. 'We'll go and help with the apple-bobbing stall.'

'Bobbing. Yes, do. Now!'

I felt neither safe nor well when I arrived at your flat that evening. I felt an attack of wind building as I took the lift up to the fourth floor, and I also had the cold–hot feeling that warns me that I'll alternate between one and the other all evening and so my brain will seize up and I will lose control and talk rubbish. Exactly what you, I'm sure, were praying I would not do.

I had bought a pineapple on the way, as a gift. They had been displayed in a pretty pyramid of yellow on a greengrocery's stall outside the Underground station.

You didn't like it, did you? It should have been a bottle of Chablis or a book. A pineapple was odd. Victoria clearly thought so.

Oh, Victoria. Victoria was slim and tall, dressed in a pencil skirt, suede ankle boots, a short grey fitted jacket and a silver choker. She had a rather tense face, but it was as beautiful as you had claimed, dammit.

'Good to meet you, Dorcas. I hear you and Jamie met in a bookshop,' she said, and steered me towards the sitting room with its huge window that looked out on a panoramic view of London. So you'd even told her that? I suddenly felt terrified that you had in fact told her everything. Anyway, where were you? *Where?* Hiding in the loo, cooking, crying in the bathroom, getting dressed, where, where? Here, we had kissed; here, we had held each other. Here, you had said that you had never felt so contained in someone as you did in me. Here, you had cried, asking again and again why we had not met earlier. Here, you had talked about Victoria, how difficult she was and yet how you still loved her. Here, you had said all the things which, written down, sound unreasonable, but which, in your voice, were not at all, they were awkward and heartfelt and complicated. And now I was here with Victoria. Your Victoria.

'You're a teacher,' she said.

'Yes.'

'Hard work.'

'Yes.'

She knew.

'Lots of marking.'

'Yes, but I don't mind marking. I find it an unpressurised way to get to know the kids. A sort of private exchange, a bit like letter-writing.'

'Letter-writing. I can see that.'

I was not sure if she could see that at all. All I *was* sure of was that my velvet trousers were too baggy and that I was, as predicted, cold. And that she most certainly *knew*.

She went on to ask me what texts I was teaching. I suddenly couldn't remember.

'*Merchant of Venice* and, um, Arthur Miller and *Merchant of Venice*, as I said, and, um, *Othello*, and yes, *Merchant of Venice*, as I said . . .'

'Favourite book at the moment?'

A deadly question. I said nothing. And suddenly, thank god, you were there.

'Well,' you trumpeted like an elephant.

Victoria and I floated uneasily down from the ceiling where we had been caught up together, in our unspoken knowing, like two moths with tangled wings.

'Sorry, Dorcas, I was on the phone to Joshua. He's on his way. Have some more wine,' you urged. 'And meet

Mark, he lectures in English with me. A fan of Coleridge, like you.'

Your eyes were so sad.

'Hello,' said Mark. 'Your name again?'

'Dorcas. I know.'

'Nothing wrong with it. I rather like it. But look, I'm so sorry, I've got to ring my wife. She's just sent me an urgent text. I'll be back.'

I was back too. With Victoria.

'Do you think you'll continue in teaching?' she asked.

'I'm not sure. I'd like to think not, but it's not an easy job to move on from. What about you?'

'What about me?'

I wasn't ready for the sharpness. 'I mean do you think you'll stick with the, er-er (!), law?'

'Well, considering I started it so late, I hardly think a change of career would be wise.'

I looked at her. She looked at me. I suddenly realised that she was aware of my age. She was so good-looking that it hadn't struck me until then how much younger I was, but I suppose even beautiful women worry.

'No, I see what you mean. It was brave of you to go through the law training.'

'Not really. Many women do it.'

'I know, but—'

'You have to be independent or you go mad.'

'Yes, I'm sure.'

I was beginning to feel uncomfortable. It was also time I introduced a topic.

145

'I like your skirt.'

'Thanks.'

'And the shirt, come to that.'

'Well.' I think she was pleased at that. 'One does one's best.'

I hate that saying: one does one's best. I decided I didn't like her, or I didn't like the her that was visible. (Later, when I glimpsed her checking her lipstick in the dark mirror of the window, I softened.)

But in that early part of the evening, I felt very badly like being rude, and for that reason became quiet, which left the floor free for you, the lecturer Mark and a couple of other friends including a lawyer called Simon Syracuse. (One fellow sufferer, then.) I won't go into it, except to say:

Point: You talked too much about books. I mean, books are important, but, Jamie, do you never just like going to sleep on an early summer evening, or entering a silent house and hearing the slowed pace of your thoughts, feeling calmed?

Point: You and Mark started quoting at each other from texts you had taught, referring to actual pages. What can one do when confronted with a page reference but listen in silence?

Point: During the cheesecake – which we had to eat standing up because it was a buffet, which you thought would be easier because then I could walk away from Victoria, but it didn't work like that, did it? – you went into Bach. Not just a passing reference, but deep into why, what, how, versions of, conductors of, recordings of. How was one meant to join in with that?

'And you, Dorcas? Which Bach is your favourite?' asked Mark.

'Um, not sure really.'

Grateful chuckle from Joshua, clearly a fan of modern music.

Point: You talked about people I didn't know.

'So sorry, Dorcas, Simon has been looking after one of my student's parents.'

'Not to worry. I'll talk to Joshua.'

Joshua was gorgeous. Thank god for Joshua. Dark-haired boy with a large nose and a baggy jumper. Big arms, big neck, strong hands, all unforced virtue. He spoke little, but seeming to gravitate towards me, I sensed he understood how I was feeling and was making himself deliberately a touch sullen to camouflage my own deficiencies. He too knew.

You began speaking very fast as if reciting some kind of social calendar, the this lecture you'd attended, the that concert, the do-you-remember-that-time-Mark type of conversation. Perhaps it was just because I was not making an effort to contribute. Perhaps, alternatively, groups of couples close into a primitive group when outsiders are about, for Mark's wife had now arrived, wearing a beautiful navy-blue trouser suit, Italian probably. Now and then, like a generous conductor, you brought me in, but I either hit the triangle so no one could hear, or did a great fart on the trombone, which brought the entire proceedings to a standstill. There was a moment when my thoughts began flowing with the ease brought on sometimes by despair. Acknowledging my interest in spirituality, you asked me what I thought of the gay bishop row currently being reported in the papers. A long and, I thought, moderately eloquent solo by myself followed; Mark and wife in blue Italian trouser suit, Simon Syracuse and woman in grey shift dress leant forward sympathetically. But Joshua, who had been my ally, suddenly became silently angry. Then he started making crude jokes. Perhaps he was disappointed that I had suddenly joined the ranks of the articulate. I tried to appreciate that the spread of food was generous, to imagine how grateful the starved and emaciated would feel with this lot in front of them. But that never works. Nothing worked. Mainly because I wanted to sit down. Well, actually, I wanted to lie down. With my face flat into the warm carpet. And cry.

I have never been so grateful to enter a lift in my life. Never. And never so in need of my late-afternoon run in the woods the next day, when I emptied out to the trees (those beings that make books but know nothing of them, nor of Bach nor wine nor politics nor bishops), I silently poured out to them all the horrors of the evening.

And when I had finished, this is what the trees reflected back to me: that you are strong; you are gentle, but your influence spreads; you had made good soil for Victoria. She was firmly settled in your life. She felt entirely secure and knew that her roots ran right under yours. Whatever you had said about me not being 'just a passing fancy', she was there to stay. Disentangling you would involve uprooting and damaging both trees.

I hate marriage. When it's someone else's.

'Miss Trevelyan?'

'What?'

'Why are you so complicated? I mean, why don't you just say Heathcliff was a psychopath instead of all that stuff about him struggling with different worlds, with education, with his crude background, with his inability to express himself, with his awkwardness and defiance of influence and stuff?'

'I'm afraid that's just how I am. It's how I think,' I said, 'and I do not wish to change. Even for the inspectors.' Neither for Inspector Hertford nor for my beloved Jamie Loring. No, not even for you.

But do you know what is saddest of all, Jamie? At the same time I realised I would not change for you, I also realised I was really ready to love you. Not to change for you, but to love you.

And you were gone.

Feedback

Paper was flying. In the last three weeks of the Christmas term, I do not remember seeing a single member of staff walking from one building to another without carrying paper. I longed for the simplicity of a finely cut figure, but even Mr Bloom, known for his linen suits and classy stage sets, was burdened by multicoloured flyers, memos, handouts, photocopies of articles. Booklets, forms, grade cards . . .

One such handout, said Our Headmistress, was to be learnt *by heart*: our 'Mission Statement'. This mission statement was a long mishmash of moral precepts concocted by the Senior Management Team. If a talented actor had had to learn this 'statement' by heart, he would have been hard-pressed, for the quantity of abstract nouns would have fuddled the most agile of brains.

Our Headmistress had asked for feedback on this document, but not until *after* the thing had been laminated.

One of its better paragraphs read: *St Edmund's College is dedicated to the pursuit of excellence whilst at the same time recognising that enjoyment and fun are central to the learning experience* comma *teachers and students alike balance these two aims by being involved in varied learning styles in lessons and avoiding the simple transmission of factual or conceptual thought.*

The saintly Lucy, tested me on this in the staff room, not allowing me to take a proper breath after the word 'experience', as the comma forbade all but a gasp. Hating it as she did, it was notable that she knew it by heart.

'What comes after the word "fun"?'

'"Central".'

'Right.'

'And the key word after "central"?'

'The.'

'That's not a key word.'

'No, right. Learning? Or would you rather experience?'

'I'll accept learning or experience for one point. I don't like this document *at all*. I would rather receive a laminated love letter.'

'Oh,' she said. 'I haven't received one of those for years.'

'Would you like me to send you one? It might cure your headaches.'

'Don't.'

*

Soon after that terrible night with Victoria, you sent me one. The love letter I needed to receive. Or you needed to send.

My love.

Was it very difficult? I know it was. Even though I reassured you. I know the evening was unpleasant for you. You must understand that, with you, as with no one else I have ever known, I have, as I've told you, an urgent desire to be known, to be seen at my best and also at my worst. You saw me that evening at my worst. Pompous and arrogant. Mr Know-all. Victoria and I frequently discourse in this vein and I know it is unattractive as well as elitist and downright rude. Would you believe me if I told you that I half did it on purpose? I wanted Victoria to feel strong, not to be threatened by you. I wanted her to feel she was cleverer than you. It will help later.

But it is you, my beloved Dorcas, whom I want as my companion. Victoria knows me to a very large extent, but not in the profound way which I realise I yearn for. Perhaps it is this urge that drives people to religion, a place where they can feel, whether it is illusory or not, that they are understood and forgiven. For me, that has never been a potent attraction, because in prayer there is no 'feedback' (hateful word). Just a rather pathetic and fumbling self-expression. I have heard religious people say that life gives them 'feedback', but for me, life's 'feedback' is too indeterminate. The fact that a nice thing happens after one has silently uttered one's moments of shame seems to me entirely, or at least possibly, incidental. I am a words man. I need to be told in words, or else viscerally.

So, my darling Dorcas, I want to ask if you would write to me and tell me all that you felt that evening. I want to know in words. Would you do that?

Jamie

I sent you a card. Inside, I wrote something like the following, for unless you have binned it, you have the original.

Jamie –

Sorry. I don't want to write about the evening with you and Victoria. You're right, I didn't enjoy it, I didn't enjoy you, I wasn't feeling very well, I felt awkward. But in hindsight, I'm pleased you asked me to meet Victoria. Now I see what I'm up against.

I am not sure how we can continue, but I know we have to.

I hope you like the card.

Love – Dorcas

*

The inspection was still a term away. A term! But the next Tuesday, after school, the staff were herded into groups of four and given another handout entitled: *Awkward Questions From Inspectors – When NOT to Answer.* We sighed, collected handfuls of consolatory biscuits and cups of coffee and went to our allotted corners.

'Now, Dorcas,' said the head of maths. 'What would you say if the inspector asked you how you would deal with a deviant member of your department who never emptied his (or her) pigeonhole or answered your notes or emails?'

Big sigh. 'I'd tell him,' I said, 'no, I'd ask him if, in all his experience of visiting departments rife with recalcitrant behaviour, he had any tips.'

'No, no,' he said. 'You can't do that. You have to think of the answer yourself. The inspector isn't an advisor, he's an inspector.'

Head of maths had commented a few days before, with a mouthful of tuna fish, that I should be a bit firmer with Pork. You're quite right, I had said. He was so pleased with my confirmation of his judgement that he spat tuna at me.

'Well, all right,' I conceded. 'But the thing is I can't think of answers six months in advance. It's like saying I will feel hot in a week, when I might in fact feel freezing.'

'No, no,' persisted head of maths. (Mr Bloom of drama and his friend Mr Latchet of music sat with amusement eating their biscuits, brushing crumbs from their linen legs.) 'No, you have to show you've been working to a strategy.'

Of course, I did have a strategy (butter him up and then smash the shit out of him) but I was not going to tell head of maths, because ... well why? I think because it suited me that he (and everyone else) thought me fragile. It meant that I wouldn't be asked to organise the Duke of Edinburgh award scheme or, failing that, be landed with the ultimate loser's responsibility: lost property. A sea of single unclaimed socks belonging to careless children.

In any case, the reason I am telling you this is because I think you were right. It was helpful to all parties that Victoria should think I was awkward, which I certainly must have appeared that evening, as well as ignorant. But do not think that I do not see life acutely. I see. I just can't speak as quickly as she can. You intentions were honourable, Jamie. I think. But the experience hurt.

Half-term

The night after the Christmas bazaar, when I had spent the afternoon on a deckchair not telling the story of dinner with Victoria, I couldn't sleep. Luckily it was a Friday so I had Saturday to be bedraggled. And, not having heard from Tanya Wright for some time, I was not in danger of having to rev myself up for another first meeting.

It was one of those nights, such as you do not suffer, Jamie, when I get into bed and know from the outset that these hours have not been scripted for sleep; they are for the mind to race about wildly like a child, while I cluck ineffectually from the sidelines, Stop it, just stop it, settle down. A regular bout of insomnia is probably the only teacher-training one really needs to know whether or not one will survive in the classroom.

That night began with a protracted re-run of a Tuesday afternoon meeting during which the staff had bickered over which children should be commended in their reports and what commendation really meant – whether it was a mark of progress or ability or the progress of ability or the ability to progress or the progression from progress to serious ability *or what*.

We then, my mind and I, transported ourselves to a departmental meeting where Pork had accused me (correctly, as it happens) of failing to tell him of a change to our scheme of work, which if he got it wrong would 'land [him] in the shit' with the inspectors. Stuffing a large forkful of mince into his mouth, he proceeded to shout wildly at the room.

I then plunged into a theme-park whizz down to the pit of my soul, where I encountered the brief and awful panic that comes from getting too close to oneself, like having one's eyes glued (literally) to a TV screen.

Do you not get *any* form of this, Jamie? I remember asking you once whether you knew the feeling of going slightly mad. You answered that you were too pragmatic for insanity but you knew other varieties of unhappiness quite well.

Where can one find peace at such times? Like you, I don't believe prayer can help. One is alone and that is that. So what is the answer? Fuck your brains out, drug them out, drink them out and then you'll sleep. Yes, I can believe all that, for it's the brain that's at fault, hiccupping about like a broken Hoover. But failing that, I have found that a good method is to use my brain in the way it likes to be used. Give it something to which it responds and then, finally, often quite quickly, it sits quiet, nerves aligned, reptilian core calmed.

So, that night, out came the notebook, the pen, the plumped-up pillows, the soft lighting of my bedside lamp. And, as I assembled these aids, I knew that the way to shift what next entered my mind to a manageable distance was to continue addressing my narrative to you. I would imagine you there. So I sat up and let my mind wander over our love and find the moment that it was looking for. And it came quite quickly to rest on those three days we spent together one half-term, when you visited the school for a day and spent two nights here.

You arrived on a warm May afternoon. I was worried that I looked tired, had not had the time to go home first and wash away the day. I knew I lacked the freshness you so like in a woman, fastidious as you are. But some wise and fair-minded side of me, like the side of you that had written of your need to be known, accepted that it was important you saw me in all states. You had watched me being inept with Joshua and Victoria, and now you were to witness me with a kind of facial shrinkage I seem to get, which simply denotes that I have expended all my energy on speech and need time to re-oxygenate my brain.

As I drove to the station, I willed my recovery time to contract into ten minutes. I thought about you holding and kissing me, I thought about you, just about you, and from time to time glimpsed my face in the mirror. Slowly it was changing, the colour returning, the cheeks filling out. Are most women so vain? Victoria: yes. Me: yes.

Well, suddenly there was no more time because there you were, with the same little black bag, but not the same stillness as before. There was less composure in your form. You were peering round, looking out. This was going to be a different kind of stay.

As usual, we were deliberately public in the car, though your hand went to my neck again, holding it gently; your indication of our status as lovers. As soon as we were inside the house, you dropped your bag and jacket on the yellow chair and we kissed. Over and over, both needing to feel and smell the other's skin.

I loved our kisses. They were so unlike the hungry mauling I had experienced from other men. We kissed as we so often talked: beginning with external matters and only much later reaching the core of what we wanted to say. It often amused me how formal you were in conversation.

On this occasion, within minutes we were upstairs lying naked on my bed, sighing with relief at the freedom we felt from all that constrained us in our day-to-day life: our commitment to good manners, to our work, to the people who were labelled our close ones. Your emotional upset had now long passed and your cock was strong and happy. As soon as you entered me, we both sighed with even deeper relief and, your face above mine, you finally asked me how I was, really how I was, as if you knew you would only hear the truth when we were connected in this way.

'I'm feeling a bit lonely,' I said. 'Everything seems focused on work.'

You pressed yourself further in and looked at me intently.

'God, I love you so much,' you said, almost helplessly.

And I felt the effort of your soul trying to find mine, to hold it, to touch and reassure it. That was what you really wanted, to feel you had entered my soul and could look into it freely. I knew that whatever I said, however honest I was, however powerful my orgasm, still I had not fully allowed you that entry. I wanted to. Oh, I so wanted to, but I have been trained in caution, and also in the beauty of singularity.

I returned your words, told you I loved you, wishing it was the true me who had said them. Perhaps I needed to hear you reiterate your love until I could really give mine. Perhaps you just *said* the words, whereas I wanted actually to plant my love inside you. Had I a cock with which to enter you, perhaps I could have said it first, for then I would have had a little of the control that I so favour and which I know is built from a predilection for solitude.

It was seven in the evening before we got up and you resumed your practical voice: 'What shall we eat? I'd like to watch the news.' I knew the pattern now and smiled to myself that I had chosen a man so much like my father in his need for order. I kissed you while you cooked, you kissed me while we ate and the news, though it had to be on, passed us both by as we watched each other rather than the stories on the Middle East. We were seated side by side on the sofa, me ending up with my head in your lap. Impervious to reporters shouting above the sound of falling bombs, my body was filled with peace. It always was when we were together in private, Jamie. You seemed to have softened my skin, brightened my eyes and I felt balanced again.

The next day you were to come to school with me to talk to my sixth form about the plays of Harold Pinter and to try out a piece of drama on a Year Seven form or, to be more precise, try out a Year Seven form on a piece of drama that you had written especially. I hadn't told anyone in the staff room of your visit. I don't know why. I don't think of myself as a suspicious person, but I didn't want anyone to pry. Students knowing you was one thing; adults are more dangerous. Their conversations are more sticky than the slick assumptions of children.

Do you remember how, even though it was only spitting, I ushered you from the car under a huge umbrella I had pilfered from the staff cloakroom, as if you were a celebrity, and sent you straight home afterwards?

I was nervous about your response to my pupils. You were used to university students who had chosen to study English, who asked, I presumed, questions which interested you, whereas my lot that year were a passive, lumpy bunch who wanted either to discuss personal issues – 'Is he your boyfriend?' – or else to listen to everything one had ever known about the plays of Harold Pinter and write it down verbatim so that one had to talk . . . like . . . this so that they could keep up, a practice that can be calming after a racy night, but becomes wearing after half an hour or so. And as for the little ones, with the lovely little scene that you had written, all week they had cavorted around the classroom in groups (I hate group work but it's the only way when they all want to play the main part) reducing your little gem to a combination of gymnastics and stand-up comedy (i.e. making up the words themselves).

I warned you.

Looking after any visitor at school is a strain. Even if you know them it is a strain, because however much you tell them, they can never know the potholes. In the main, they put their feet firmly in all of them.

Do you remember that Pinter session? The rain had stopped and the sun had come out and, forgetting that you dislike direct sunlight, I suggested we go outside and sit in the lovely orchard that backs on to the English block. I brought you no Panama hat, no deckchair or water. You sat on the rug that one of the girls had been instructed to bring.

We women spent a long time organising ourselves, to be frank more interested in our physical arrangements than in getting to grips with *The Homecoming*. We didn't much care if the play was pretentious or profound, we wanted only the soft sound of the summer trees and the feel of our bare legs on the woollen blanket. We lay in a star formation, while you, for whom we had finally realised a chair was needed, sat above us, doing little to control your straying eyes.

'So, what do you think of Ruth?' you asked the star.

Giggles. Much munching of doughnuts.

'These are still hot. Did you get them on the way to school?'

'My mum did. I sat in the car.'

'You have been asked,' I said, feeling embarrassed, 'about *Ruth*.' (I worry sometimes that nearly ten years of teaching has made me emphatic in ordinary conversation. Do you think it has?)

A flurry of vague comments followed about Ruth's coldness, her references to living in a place full of rocks and so being a victim of a barren life in America et cetera, but texts, those vital props for intelligent discussion, remained closed on the grass.

'And what,' you tried again, 'do you think of the scene with the glass of water?'

More on Ruth being cold and yet a bit of a 'slut', and 'How can she begin to have it off with Joey?' But soon the questions faded out as we all became hazy in the sunlight and could summon no evidence for our answers. No one wanted to think and somehow, with you being so serious, there was afoot a collective urge to tease you. I could see you struggling with the heat but instead of moving the session inside, I let it slide on into the inevitable: you giving a lecture, a very long and exquisite lecture, which I enjoyed enormously, because I learnt so much. It should have been you and I alone seated under a tree. This particular bunch of girls needed only to learn about *their* sexuality, what was attractive about *themselves*, and whether you fancied them. They were lost to everything else.

When you had finished and they were busy plucking daisies and twiddling their young fingers around blades of grass, I felt overwhelmed by a sort of protective love for you. I had wanted so much to show you off to my sweet, inept sixth formers, but to them you were only another teacher.

'I've got a bugger of a headache,' you said, once I'd shooed them away and they'd stood up and moved off sleepily, covered in grass. We had a few minutes on our own in the classroom and I plied you with water and painkillers. And in those very moments when I most loved you, you were folded away, protecting yourself. Perhaps I should have taken this as a warning.

The second group made you smile. You left it to me to organise them and this time the hour consisted of much movement and a hell of a lot of arguing. Understanding that they were being watched by the actual writer of the scene, these twelve-year-olds became furious with each other. They had left the entire piece behind them, together with all other concerns; they were still at that endearing stage when each week is binned with the garbage on a Friday evening and whatever was learnt three days earlier has to be begun again.

They also had terrible trouble following the lines of the script while moving about. As a result, many cock-ups occurred.

I decided, having learnt from the first mess, to have them move the desks back, sit down and spend the last fifteen minutes talking to you. How kind you were to them, asking them their names and telling them that names were important and they should look up their origins.

'My name's Portia,' shouted Portia. 'But Miss Trevelyan calls me Clementine, because she says I look like an orange.'

'No, it's because you're sweet,' I explained.

You looked confused by that. The classroom isn't for silly affections. It is for etymology and dictionary definitions and comparisons and explanations. You went to the board and wrote the words *Aaron Todd*.

'Say I was called that.'

'Are you?'

'That doesn't matter. This is a thought experiment.' (I have noticed as a teacher that girls generally dislike thought experiments; they prefer what is real and tender.) 'What do you think it means?'

'Aaron is someone in the bible with a rod.'

'Well, ye-es,' you said, adopting that slow, patient voice which you must have used with Joshua when he was learning to read. 'But in fact, the name Aaron means "a light". Aaron – "a light" or, alternatively, "exalted". And Todd?'

'He's a policeman on telly,' said the girl who had

been the major cock-up culprit in your lovely little script.

'Ye-es,' you repeated. 'But what about if you said "on your tod"? What would that mean?'

'On your own,' shouted the culprit, much happier with improvisation.

'Exactly. However, in German the word *tod* means "death". So the name in full means: "a light on its own in death" or "exalted in death".'

They didn't like this. They didn't want to hear unhappy things. They did not want your sadness, your death, your aloneness. They wanted to hear about your being a professor and wearing a mortar board and living in London in a luxurious flat, being rich and having lots of children. 'Yes, I have one,' you answered, when they asked. 'Joshua.'

'What does he do and what does your wife do?'

So they weren't satisfied with a piece of you, certainly not a sad slice of you, a theme within you. No. They wanted Daddy and Mummy and Joshua. Only that would do. Like most children, they needed to construct you in their chosen image. As do you me? I you? Do we all do that? And, my darling Jamie, is that where our real problem lies?

Perhaps it was the relief of being away from them, the same relief that I feel every day as I step back into the privacy of my house, that led to what happened next.

'I feel like a gin and tonic,' you said, as if it were

something you never normally felt like. Then you paused, puzzled at yourself. 'And a cigarette.' I knew what you meant. The day had been tricky and you needed the help of a bit of astute self-indulgence. We walked to the Indian supermarket at the end of the road, witnessed a shouting match in Punjabi between Mataji and Mr-ji, and purchased our sins.

I hadn't smoked a cigarette for over fifteen years. But this one, coming as it did *with you*, was gorgeous. Forbidden-gorgeous, child-aping-adult-gorgeous. The gin similarly. I have told you this before, but that was one of the loveliest moments I have shared with you. So often, one comes away from events which have dislocated the spirit alone and, slowly, like an animal sniffing out comfort, one comes eventually upon the thing that helps: the particular food, activity, voice. And if it is a voice, one pleads with it to synchronise with one's own and then raise a note and fill out its tone. We found the right note together and it brought not just relief but laughter: you inhaling deeply and me puffing at the fag like a nervous thirteen-year-old.

Definition of death-state: a cigarette alone.

Definition of resurrection: a cigarette – only one, only once – together.

'Will you leave me?' I asked you in bed. I was still deeply suspicious of men, clever men, maybe because I was unsure of my own staying power. Once, when I was a child, a teacher at school, whom I loved, said as she watched me falter at the end of a hundred-metre race, 'Dorcas is someone who always gives up just before the end.' I don't know how I know she said it, but she did and it has cursed me. Teachers should be careful.

You were quiet for a moment. Resting. You had done all your speaking during the day. After making love, you were tired. Perhaps that's why I asked you then. When people are tired, either they cannot be bothered to tell the truth or they cannot be bothered to lie.

Whichever, you put out your hand and held my breast. And, as if this were the last action you could possibly manage, you said, 'I don't know. I don't know what we are and where we are going. I can't think about it now. Wait a little, my darling. Not now. We always leave people in the end. For the moment, we are here.'

Why did I feel happy, no, not happy, but quiet, contented, rather than fobbed off when you said that? I have spent my life stretching beyond myself to be good and do not know myself as I am, therefore. I know myself as I ought to be. Your words brought me to where we actually were. Then. At that exact moment.

I have always loved your voice. It calmed me from the beginning. When I heard it that day in Hatchards, it was like an outstretched rescuing hand.

We slept for a few hours. You regained your energy. At four, we both woke and I thought we would make love again. But you had remembered my question. 'Turn towards me,' you said.

And we lay on our sides face to face. It was already

light enough to see each other. I wanted to sort out your hair before we spoke, smooth it down, bring your body back from sleep. You closed your eyes as I mothered you for a moment and then you began.

'I am nineteen years older than you.'

'Not that again, Jamie.'

'But think of it, Dorcas. When you were born, I was nineteen. Older men always, or often at least, want young women, even young men, for a particular reason. They bring them alive. You have done that to me. I was dying. My marriage looks reasonable when it needs to, glamorous even in certain lights; it can look fine at a dinner party, for instance. But I have been dying for some time. Too successful in a way. Too able. Everything there and yet nothing there at all. When I saw you in the bookshop and then we had coffee, I thought you beautiful in a strange, quivering sort of way. I could see you were sensitive, that you changed from moment to moment. You don't like that about yourself, Dorcas, but it is a way of being alive. I go to Hatchards and I buy my books and I know how I'll feel, I know what will please me, I know where I'll have coffee afterwards, I know where I'll go next. I could see you didn't know. Each moment for you was a possibility and it still is. I don't want to fix you so much that you don't live any more. I don't want to kill you. Permanence is a kind of death. Do you see that? You don't want to die, do you?'

'I think I do,' I told you. 'Yes, I *do* want to die.' I was

169

getting excited now. 'I feel as if I have been moving fast for a very long time, for years and years, and now I want to be still. I'd like to do what we said on the phone in those first weeks when you were abroad. To marry you on a boat and live quietly with you. And be still. I'm tired.'

I could feel tears coming, spilling, falling. I was shaking with the awareness of how tired I was of being so acutely alive.

Those lovely arms again. You steered me with your arm towards the restaurant for that first coffee and now your arm steered me towards your shoulder as you heaved yourself on to your back. Slowly, very slowly, you stroked my hair.

'My darling,' you said, 'my darling.'

And I felt my whole childhood well up and out of me. Each stroke of my hair brought another memory. Such terrible grief. And you had it too. But, during both sex and upset, we had come to understand that it works better if one person is attended to at a time.

'So. You want me to kill you.' Your voice had a smile in it.

'Yes please. Now, if possible.'

'I see. And what would be your preferred method?'

'I'd like,' I said loudly, 'I'd like you to buy a big flat, *not* with black leather armchairs, a flat with soft colours. Wooden furniture, no carpets, expensive rugs. But warm. A big bed. A huge bed, in fact. Near the sea. Beside the sea. In fact, on the beach itself. So no, not a flat, a house with a bay window. Sea view. And I'd like you to put me in a bubbling spring.'

'What about the sea?'

'No, no, a spring in the garden in a slatted tub, flavoured with herbs. Mint. Lemon verbena. Then I'd like you to dry me and carry me up to the big bed, the *huge* bed with white cotton duvet, thin duvet, duck-down, and I'd like you to lie me down in bed and fuck me gently and then just afterwards I'd like you to inject me with some fabulous drug that would send me to sleep for about three years. And while I was asleep—'

'Stop it, Dorcas. *Stop it.*'

'Why? Then, while I was asleep, you'd—'

'No, don't.' And you got out of bed. 'I'm going for a pee.'

And suddenly I knew that you would leave me. You wanted me alive, so you were not in my bed any more. As you aren't now. And now I understand. I understand why you left me. And I see your wisdom in doing so. And if I could only know the end of the story, I could rest. But I don't. I just know you have left me to live.

This is a horrible experience.

Extra-curricular Activities

In compiling my slimline handbook, I wrote Our Head-mistress an email asking her what 'Contribution To The Community' meant. This was a subheading in the Annual Departmental Plan. Is it, I asked, things like patronising the local Indian shop rather than Tesco's? Is it talking to children about 'deep issues'? Is it . . . Well, what is it, in fact? I am sure that, as a department, we already do much of it, if I did but know what *it* was. She replied curtly: *Dorcas, first of all, please learn to use the school email system correctly. When I receive an email from you, it dates back six months. Go to Sent, delete Sent, then go to New, Open Doc, then Create New. Thank you. Now regarding ECAs. SMT define ECAs as anything from CTC to CTS to CTG. In other words, Lucy* [my patron saint] *could list the school magazine, Bill* [Pork] *could put down football and you – what? – massage?*

As you see, my preferred ECA is conducted lying

down, being massaged, doing sod all, though I was offended by this reference especially its rude little insertion – what? – because I *do* run several other activities that are more erudite than bringing in a masseur from a clinic in Forest Row to serve the weary, and these should have sprung first to her mind.

The thing is that, like you, I don't really believe in ECAs. They sound like a form of treatment for the mentally ill, though I know they are meant to stave off insanity. And death?

(I am filled still with the image of Victoria in her pencil skirt. I am afraid of her, Jamie. I am afraid of her even being on the same planet as me. I don't want to die at all. All that stuff about being drugged on a beach or in a herbal pool was rubbish. It is her I want to see floating out to sea. Sorry, but that's my current unspeakable but write-able thought.)

Well, if St Edmund's College was going to inflict activity upon me from above, flinging down after-school clubs by the dozen until my head reeled with debates, book circles, discussion groups, then I was certainly going to preserve the weekends for unadulterated inactivity.

It was early in the new year that Tanya Wright rang. Tinged with seasonal joy perhaps, she jollied on about 'a delightful man who I think would *really suit you*. He likes walking, pubs, reading, theatre, going abroad and life drawing.'

I hesitated. Then lied with absolute confidence: 'I've

just met someone else.' Ms Wright sounded disappointed. *I see everyone personally. I bring love and light into
people's lives. I have attended over one hundred weddings.* I
pictured the top of her towelling trousers tight around
her Christmas tummy.

'Congratulations.'

'I'm terribly sorry,' I said, simpering awkwardly, 'but –
um – can I have some of my money back as I haven't
met my full quota of men?'

'I'm afraid not, and besides, you never know what
might happen. Best to keep all options open. Have to
dash.'

This made me cross, but because with the single word
'just' ('I've *just* met someone else') I had told a lie.
There was no one else except you. Oh well, sod it! Let
her keep her money. And let me keep you, the only
person who would not force upon me the distracting outdoor activities enumerated by Ms Wright, with which so
many wile their lives away.

In that little hesitation with Tanya Wright I did not consciously decide to lie, I just took a breath and out came
the words. I do this quite often. Not to myself. I am
afflicted with a nit-picking conscience, but it seems to
react adversely only to self-deception. It cares much less
about what is said to anyone else, unless the words have
clearly caused hurt. It does flair up, however, in unexpected ways. As a child, when once asked by a teacher
who had written some unpleasant smut on the board, I

certainly didn't confess. But later, much later, a week, two weeks, when the victim had forgotten the crime, I slunk up, after a sleepless night, and said not that it was me who had done it, because it wasn't, but that it was me who had found the chalks with which the act had been perpetrated.

I was worried about this. And even more worried when my offence wasn't recognised. Perhaps it was then that I began to realise that people on the whole tend not to care if you lie. Indeed, they tend not to care about you at all. As a child, I thought that I was on everyone's mind all the time, that they loved and fretted about me and that I generally occupied their entire mental life. I not infrequently daydreamed of my funeral and all the crying that would go on. Lucy told me that this is a known psychological phenomenon in children. Have you ever done that daydreaming thing, Jamie? I bet you haven't. Maybe that's because you rather like to think of yourself as inferior, just so that you can keep on being pleasantly surprised by all the accolades you receive.

Anyway, what I'm trying to say is that, for me, lying has often felt like the least time-consuming thing to do, but from the moment I knew you, I saw that you did not do this, though you claimed you did. It was more a feeling than anything else that told me that you were a truthful being, or at least a very bad liar.

What I want you to know is that day after day, both when we were together and apart, when we were just writing, talking on the phone or in each other's presence,

I could feel your truth working inside me as if you had impregnated me with your weight and were gently drawing me down to earth, to the solid ground where a slab is a slab, a sod is a sod.

Do you remember the time you told me about how you had been to bed with that woman who looked after you on your visit to India?

'Jamie.'

'What?' you barked. You were fiddling with a biro.

'You know you promised to tell me your sexual history, well, we've got to the bit when you were going to Calcutta.'

'I hate India.'

'You *like* to hate India. It gives you pleasure to do so.'

'Well?'

'We-ell.'

And you opened your eyes and came to sit opposite me, the oblong of London night beside us again through the half-drawn curtains.

'Are you sure you want to know, Dorcas?'

'Yes, in detail. With photos to accompany, if possible.'

'Don't be silly.'

'All right, no silliness.' And I settled myself cross-legged like a little Buddha, awaiting your confession.

'Well,' you began, stretching out your legs and rubbing your eyes with your fists, 'it had been a ghastly day. The arrangements had been cocked up, as usual. Lecture scheduled for ten, no one there until eleven, sound equipment making obscene noises throughout, no air conditioning, endless questions of an astonishingly incoherent kind asked in pre-war-style English and so on and so on and so on.'

'No, don't go "and so on". Nor "and so forth" either. Tell me the details.'

'Well . . . my minder was a woman called Natalia. Very intelligent. Works for Longman, lived in a nicely done-up flat. A huge contrast to anything outside. Cool, sparsely furnished, miraculously quiet. Very good taste. And her husband, David, is a delightful man. Works for the BBC out there. Very good job and all that.'

'Yes . . .'

'Well, we dined and so on.' (I smiled.) 'I was very tired and, I suppose, so relieved to be away from the wretched university and all its nonsense that I was a little out of control.'

'How old were you?'

'Oh well, this was a few years ago, so what, about forty-four? Anyway, they had this vast sofa, I mean vast, and after dinner, I made a move to start washing-up and was severely reprimanded and told that the servants did all that. Then we sat, the three of us side by side, and watched the news and a bit of a rather good film, I forget what. I was next to David. That is, David was in the middle.'

'Draw a diagram.'

'Stop it. David was in the middle. He had his arm around Natalia and at some point' – here you cocked your head, wanting the exact moment, but unable to

177

find it – 'he slid his other arm around my shoulder. Now I have never had a leaning in that direction. Have you, by the way? Have you ever liked a woman?' No answer. 'In any case, I had this sudden desire to kiss him. It was really most extraordinary. Anyway, Talia went up to bed quite soon after this. She is a perceptive woman, but in that gentle way that often gets mistaken for shyness or innocence. Rather like you, as a matter of a fact. So there we were, on the sofa, side by side and so on.'

I smiled again.

'And I realised that David reciprocated the feeling, because his hand moved to my knee. Well, we sat, and we sat, and we went on sitting. And then – I remember this graphically – David asked, "Do you like playing golf?" "Certainly not," I shot back in disgust. "Why, do you?" "Never." And then, we turned towards each other and kissed. And my god, the excitement was quite extraordinary.'

'I thought this was about Natalia, not her husband. Woah!' I heard the intonations of my students in my voice, and disliked myself.

'Well, the long and the short of it was—'

'No, Jamie, not the long and the short, *all of it*.'

'We-ell, we said something along the lines—'

'Not along the lines. *What exactly?*'

'Oh, I don't know. Time for bed or something like that. And I said yes and he then said with complete composure, "I'd like you to sleep with us. Would you like that?" I was utterly taken aback, but realised that I "would like that" very much. I asked about Natalia, was told that she would also "like that very much", that they had in fact discussed it earlier in the evening.'

Looking back, I realise that I was in fact hurt by this revelation. But I was also amused, shocked, intrigued. Hence my stunning question: 'Did he put it up your bottom?'

'Dorcas.'

'Well, he could have.'

'Well, he didn't. No.'

'So who did what to who?'

'Whom.'

'All right, whom to whom. *Come on!*'

'I think it went: D to T, me watching.'

'How, how?'

'Stop it. D to me, T watching, T to me, D watching.'

'Which did you like best?'

'You're meant to be upset.'

'Not a bit. Which was best?'

'Well, interestingly – of course marvellous watching them at it – but actually David and I. Perhaps because it was new.'

'Did you have an orgasm?'

'Of course.'

'Did you all?'

'Of course.'

'So you're a homosexual, in fact.'

'Not a bit.'

'Yes, you are. What about that young man you told me about?'

'That was different.'

And you scooped me, cross-legged and all, off my chair and on to your lap. 'I am queer, yes, but I have done nothing of that nature since, and I love women. And . . . I am in love with you. I am surprised by it, but I am. Totally.'

I started laughing.

'Dorcas.'

'What?'

'Why are you laughing?'

'I don't know. I feel nervous.'

But I knew you weren't lying.

'Dorcas.'

I was sitting in the staff dining room eating lunch and reading a book, trying to avoid the noise.

'Aren't you meant . . . ?'

'Meant what?'

'Meant to be doing your discussion group thing? They're waiting for you, but the chaplain's there, she's started it.' It was Lucy again, she of the pale-blue trouser suits, of the gentle nudges towards professionalism.

'Do you think she could manage it on her own? I'm loving this book so much, Lucy. Could you tell her I'm in sick bay, you know, I've fainted or something?' Then I remembered that Lucy had once said that she couldn't recall having told a lie in her life.

'I should just not turn up. You've missed half of it already,' she said.

She left the room quietly and I suddenly started worrying. I was trying, together with the head of art, drama and several other unappreciated experts, to get through the pay 'threshold'. We had all laughed about it. It sounded like being admitted into heaven, a particular heaven for which we had to fill in a complicated form, worth a hundred or so more pounds pay a month. Did not turning up for extra-curricular activities mean I might not make it through? What I wanted of course was to be carried across the threshold in the arms of a fat little inspector as he purred, 'You are *undoubtedly* gifted and thus deserve a reward.'

'Have you by, the way? Have you ever liked a woman?'

My excuse for not answering was that you were in the full flow of your own story, but later, when we were talking about my sexual history, I deliberately omitted one incident.

I do, still, feel nervous about it. But here goes. Three doors down from me lives a twenty-seven-year-old woman called Sophie. It is her first house. She is already twice as rich as me because she is a successful businesswoman and works in London. She has a boyfriend there and they are in the process of selling houses and settling in Hammersmith, though she likes it here.

Sophie and I used to run together, especially in the autumn and through the winter months when going alone was dangerous. We both preferred the woods to the road, not least because we wished to preserve our knees into old age. For a stretch, we would go every day, then forget, and then resume. Our arrangements were entirely instinctive and we never socialised beyond this.

Sophie is even taller than me, with one of those un-exaggerated faces – features well spread out, good skin – that one looks at with simple appreciation. Not stunning eyes or a sexy mouth or anything like that, just simple and resilient. A face that can stand up to tiredness. I used to watch her sometimes walking to her car in the morning and envied how elegant she looked even in the most modest of clothes.

One day, late in October, we set off running at about half past four. We took our usual route, down by the school, through the churchyard, up a steep hill – running towards the sun – and then in a circle around the woods. Two, three miles perhaps. Sometimes, when we had been running for a while and become tired, we'd just stop and lean against a couple of trees. It was natural at these moments for us to tell each other quite personal things about our bodies, our men, anything. Sometimes, we'd hold hands, one pulling the other along for encouragement. Once out of the woods and back on the road – Jane Austen got it right about things happening when you are beyond sight of your house – we would resume pleasantries, until we reached my front door where we reverted to being mere neighbours. I never invited Sophie in.

Perhaps it was this clear, unspoken arrangement that gave us the freedom to be so intimate that day. As we set out it was drizzling, but the sun was shining at the same time in that indecisive combination typical of our island. I was running ahead of Sophie. She called out that I was fitter than her. I explained without stopping that I had just drunk a strong cup of coffee. I was running on nervous not real energy. We weren't competitive. Sometimes she ran ahead, sometimes me, but today I could tell she was tired. We kept going up the hill, stopping a couple of times, but only for a few seconds. Then we turned the corner and I stopped and bent down to sort out my shoelace. Sophie ran on. She was loping rather, but still, as always, I envied the straightness of her back, the square cut of her shoulders and her half-Turkish toffee skin.

It was halfway along the home straight of the woods that I casually bent to tie my shoelace for a second time. This time, Sophie stopped and waited. When I stood up, she looked different. No, actually, she didn't look different, she *was* different. In one second, she had changed, become personal, angry, something – what?

'Why don't you just get some new trainers?'

'I don't *want* new trainers.'

'Well, new laces, new *something*.'

New something or was it old something? Whatever it was, the air between us was no longer neutral.

'Sorry,' she mumbled.

As I said earlier, we often caught hands for a minute.

This time, we ran for about fifty metres squashed together along the narrow path, helping each other through the brambles and nettles, her hand in mine.

'Not so fast,' I said. 'I thought you were tired.'

I began to feel strange then. I knew something was happening but it was not anything I could articulate. I absolutely could not say it or ask it. And that was the beauty of it. Neither of us was in charge. I cannot remember that feeling with a man. And our turning towards each other was just as if the wind had blown us that way. We looked at each other and she put her hand on my back. That warm hand. Her other hand went to my bottom. And mine, where, where? To her face. I held her head in my two hands, felt her dark hair, then her cheeks. Between us, we drew our whole selves together and kissed. A long, unsearching, almost still kiss. The sensation of each other's lips. A woman's lips.

It was close to being dark. There was and never is anyone in sight in the woods. And still no words. We knew what we wanted. To take off our T-shirts, anything restricting, concealing, tight, and to kiss again. My god, that skin, the erect nipples, the softness of Sophie's neck. We rubbed at each other, kissed freely now. But that wasn't enough. The darkness seemed to allow anything, to urge us to go on, go on.

But for a moment, we stopped. Five minutes further on, there is a small stream and an inlet where there are no trees. There were other prickly things no doubt, but we needed to lie down and we needed to be naked.

She was the first to undress. I followed and eased myself down on to her, shifting and moving until I could feel the soft hair between her legs against mine. But I was too heavy for the light touch that we both knew we wanted. She turned to the side, I clamped my legs around her waist, wishing, yes I remember this, wishing that she had a cock with which to enter me. But the gentle rain, the darkness, the silence, the skin, that skin, Jamie, the firm, small roundness of her breasts – so unshowy, so, yes, so unspecial and for that so lovely – and the new-oldness of all of these sensations had us calling out within seconds.

I am sure if I read a book, if I read in some hand-book (!) about this activity – definitely extra-curricular – there would be some term for this kind of orgasm. I can only tell you that it came from inside, deep up, up inside and travelled down, down and out into her and on to her and through her into the ground. And while it was happening, everything felt as if it was moving, we must have been moving, I know, yet it was also so still, so quiet.

After that, something in us wanted to stand up and leave our clothes there. Of course, we couldn't, so we bundled up our stuff and walked, our arms around each other. But I left my shoes. (I have seen them since, deep in the grass under the trees.)

We both had boyfriends. We did not need to speak about our love for either of them; we needed only to feel innocently deviant and we wanted to do what we had done again. Which we did. Twice. But it wasn't the same for me. I don't know why. Perhaps because it was arranged, whereas that first and really only time, simply occurred.

Sophie didn't feel the same. She wanted to go on. I told her it felt wrong.

'Why?'

'I don't know.'

I've found this always to be the safest answer. No one can argue with a hunch.

I do wonder what you are doing at this moment. I miss your laughter, your way of putting my seriousness into perspective. I may joke about school, but the constant earnest focus on trivia does genuinely get me down. If you were here, you would help me out of it. I know you would. Perhaps I am learning to help myself. Don't laugh. I can hear you laughing at my obsession with moral improvement. It is not a bit funny. I have lost half a stone since we last saw each other.

Religious Education

There are days when the adrenalin levels at school are so high that one feels as if one is moving around a sort of booze-crazed nightclub. Sometimes, without you to intervene, I cannot dissociate myself from school at all and at other times I feel so distant from it that I can almost measure the hysteria like a doctor checking blood pressure.

Last week, Mrs Warhole, the head of religious education, took assembly. She came in and, as if addressing an audience hard of hearing, loudly enunciated, 'Good morning, girls. My assembly is about the truth.' On the screen was a film star I didn't recognise and everyone else did. 'As you know,' she said, 'X (film star) always says in X (film): "The Truth is Out There". And, girls, it is. The truth *is* out there.'

I sat back with a stupid glimmer of hope that she might guide us to where The Truth Out There was. But no. She just said, 'I repeat, The Truth is Out There.'

This time with a slightly different emphasis. As if that was a clue. Teachers are very bad like that. They tell you that things exist. They pose the why and then answer it with a what or a when or another why.

'And in order to illustrate my point, I am going to conduct a contest between Our Headmistress and Mr Bister. So a round of applause for Our Headmistress and Mr Bister.'

The applause followed.

'Stand here, Mr Bister,' she said, with a bossy pout on her, 'and you here, Headmistress. That's right. And now watch the screen.' Then up came an image of a woman in a pink dress, back to the camera, carrying a soft toy. 'Is,' she said emphatically, 'that me? Remember, The Truth is Out There.'

Mr Bister (Pork to me) and Our Headmistress each had to vote and had been primed to contradict one another, so Pork said it was her and Our Headmistress said it wasn't.

'Wrong, Mr Bister. I hated cuddly toys. So one point to Our Headmistress. Now, a slight variation. I am going to ask you a question that is about me and you are going to say yes or no. Would I or would I not have worn turquoise to my thirtieth birthday party?'

'You can't answer yes or no to that,' asserted Pork, picking his knees up as if to begin a can-can.

'All right, clever clogs, but I repeat would I – yes – or would I not – no – have worn turquoise to my thirtieth birthday party?'

'You would, YES,' shouted Pork.

'And I don't think you would, NO,' said Our Headmistress.

Then up came a slide of Mrs Warhole in a turquoise silk top, looking slightly pissed, leaning towards a large man whom we all nosily studied.

'One point to Mr Bister.'

I won't go on, Jamie. You get the drift. She concluded: 'So you see, the truth is out there if you think hard. And now let us pray: 'Dear God, please help us to seek the truth throughout our lives and please help us to find it wherever it may be *out there*. Amen.'

Huge applause. Our Headmistress all smiles and congratulations, her bosoms setting off for the lectern, thrilled that this had put everyone in a sufficiently good mood to accept her rebuke about loo paper stuffed down the toilets (why not toilet paper stuffed down the toilets?) and a general glut of litter, which 'I do NOT want to see again, do you HEAR?'

Oh yes, we hear.

The next day Mrs Warhole was away, sick. I think she tires herself out playing this constantly ebullient role. Anyway, it meant I had to cover her RE lesson, in a classroom that is a cross between a new age shop in Covent Garden and the haberdashery department of Debenhams.

Maybe I am wrong about Mr Hereford. Maybe he will be a nice man, after all. Maybe he'll be charming, and jaded by educational practices, and generous in his judgements, upsetting our collective image of inspectors as murderers with stockings over their heads wielding twenty-four-carat gold fountain pens.

Mrs Warhole's instructions for her cover lesson went as follows: *Girls are to begin writing an essay titled: There is never a case for adultery. To what extent do you agree? They should complete this in the double lesson.* I had always thought RE an easy option, but seventy minutes to settle the state of at least a third of the Western world seemed a tall order.

'What does "to what extent" mean?' said one girl, another way of saying: I'm not in the mood, I'd rather be riding my horse.

'It's easy,' said another, a member of Mrs Warhole's Christian Union. 'Adultery's wrong.'

'What?'

I hadn't been listening. I had set aside this particular double lesson for some paperwork which the senior mistress had been demanding for a couple of months now.

'Adultery's wrong,' repeated the Christian.

'Well,' I said reluctantly, 'it's always a good idea to acknowledge the arguments on the other side as well.'

The girls shuffled about in that way animals do when they aren't going to leave you alone. I reluctantly began to accept the fact that the senior mistress would have to have one more sleepless night awaiting her forms about examination entries.

'There's no other side to adultery,' the Christian said.

'Well,' I began. 'Suppose two people have stopped loving each other and deep down they both know it—'

'Then they should get a divorce before they do adultery.'

'That can take time.'

'Then they should wait.'

'Why?' put in another child, who was casually swanning her way through a life of separated parents with multiple partners, remarriages, step-, half-, once-, twice-removed siblings and god knows what else. 'Ah, bloody hell, I think they should just get on with it,' she sneered.

'Have you told Victoria?'

Do you remember me finally asking you this, when we were reading together in your flat one afternoon, the flat that *both* of you owned? I had noticed that this was one of the best times to speak to you, when you were reading. When involved in a good book, you would often raise your face to me as if you were in touch with a part of your consciousness that allowed you more possibilities than were available when you were cooking, say. When you were cooking, you were *fascistic* both with the knife and your views.

'What?' You weren't deaf, but I think you quite liked pretending to be. I did not repeat the question.

'I haven't told her but she knows.'

'Why don't you talk to her about it, Jamie? Wouldn't you feel better?'

'I don't know.'

'If we were married and I was having an affair, I would tell you.'

'How do you know you would?'

'Because there is something in your nature which brings out the truth.'

'Ah, but with Victoria, it's different. It's as if she wouldn't want to know, as if she wants to keep everything as it is. I've told you already that there's something atrophied in our marriage which means it wouldn't make any difference, and yet . . .'

'I can't believe that, Jamie, though I know you mean it. What I think is that there's something linking you two that neither of you want to break. You love each other but you've also outgrown each other. But when old age comes, it will be all right again. It's the middle period when you need to be free, almost as a means of saving yourself for when old age does come. Isn't that right?'

'How can you say that without anger, Dorcas?'

'Because I love you and I know you and I'm not an idealist about worldly arrangements. I know there have to be arrangements.'

'My dear love . . .'

I remember the look of gratitude on your face. That someone should be so tolerant of an injustice. You pulled me with sudden force from my chair, held me to your chest and stroked my hair.

'I worry about you, in the night,' you said. 'I worry about us. Don't think I don't.' And you forced my head away from you, your eyes burning into mine, your hands hard against my face.

'Yes, I do know, Jamie. I know you love me.'

'Why are you so calm then? *Why?*'

'I don't know.' And I didn't.

'A divorce can take time,' I said again to the Christian. 'And in the process, it can destroy so much.'

'What do you mean?' she asked. 'Surely everything is already destroyed by then anyway.'

I had been calm during that conversation with you but, later, afterwards, and particularly at this moment, when I was with this little gaggle and half wanted to be married with them as my children, I felt sad and hard done by.

My piano teacher used to tell me that my timing was atrocious. She was right. It is the case in everything. If there is a given moment when we are sent to heaven or hell, that's when I'll be out shopping. I was hurting too late, too late to show you, and that omission was what was hurting me now and fuelling this lesson. The wounded can teach well.

'Sometimes,' I said slowly, 'when a person is having an affair and there is something right about it, right almost *because* it is unlawful, and not part of what society applauds—'

'I don't think anything unlawful can be right,' said the Christian.

'No, I agree with you,' I went on. 'And somehow the

most *unlawful* thing to do with a precious experience is to publicise it – worse, to try to label it.'

'But surely it won't last then, will it?' blurted out Holly, a girl who wore only designer clothes.

'Why not?'

'Because you won't know what it is, you won't know if you can rely on it.'

'I bet you don't know the name of that tree,' I said.

'Oak, innit?' Holly smiled, arms crossed, large make-up bag masked as pencil case in front of her as protection from prying teachers.

'Actually, I haven't a clue,' I replied, 'and nor do I care. It's probably been there for about a hundred years. And does *it* know its name?'

Sniggers.

'It doesn't know its name, you don't know its name, I don't know its name, but it's lasted. So what's the difference if you give it a label?'

'Lots,' said Holly, twiddling her blonde curls. (Though she was hooked on hair straighteners, which were also in the pencil case, pretending to be scissors.)

'I still think it's wrong,' said the Christian.

'And I don't know how a relationship can last if it doesn't move forward. It's got to become something, dunnit,' Holly went on.

'Has the tree moved? Has the tree got on a plane and gone off to Miami for a holiday? Taken a business-class seat and stretched out its roots and asked for a drink of sap?'

'Stop going on about the tree, Miss Trevelyan.'

'All right then. I'll tell you something about me.'

Nudges.

'Hey, Miss Trevelyan, did you see the dally larma last night? The head of the buddhas in Tibet?'

'Not personally, no. You mean the Dalai Lama. He lives in India.'

'He kept giggling and talking about going to the toilet. I thought he was stupid.'

'Shut up. Let Miss Trevelyan tell her thing about herself.'

'It has a Buddhist flavour to it, as a matter of a fact.'

'Oh no.'

'Oh yes. I lived with this guy in London about ten years ago. We were together for five years. Very close, loved each other, all that, didn't marry, don't know why not.'

'Why not?'

'I told you, I don't know. But—'

'Why didn't you, if you loved each other?'

'Just wait. Let her tell it.'

'What did he look like?'

'That isn't relevant.'

'I bet he had a ponytail.'

'He didn't, but *anyway*. A moment came when we both knew it should end. We could have married, we could have had children, but in some way, that's what would have ended it, made it artificial, public. One evening, we went out for dinner and it turned out—'

'What did you have to eat? I bet you had nut roast and—'

'Shut *up*.' (The Christian.)

'It turned out that we were both planning to say the same thing: that we wanted to end it in order to preserve it. Which we did. And we haven't seen each other since or spoken. We deliberately kept our silence and yet strangely that has kept it alive, which is, as I say, a very Buddhist thing to do.'

'You're *weird*.'

'I understand,' came a little voice from the back.

It was a tiny girl with watery eyes called Jessica, who had not yet met puberty. I was fond of her. Her vocabulary always touched me. It was quaint, adventurous, and her body looked as perfectly proportioned as her mind. The other girls also liked her, because she was artistic in a way that they envied and also they could see that one day she would be beautiful.

'Do you?' I asked gently.

'Yes. Because, because we had a dog called Deerstalker.'

'Was he a Buddhist?'

'Stop it. And, Jessica?' I encouraged, trying not to join in with the general mirth.

'And she got cancer of the rectum,' she announced with dignity. 'And she, Deerstalker I mean, could have had treatment, which would have been like your label.'

'That's like calling marriage an illness,' blurted out the Christian.

'No, you idiot, the treatment's like marriage. What Jess means is that treatment is unnatural. She wanted Deerstalker to be natural like Miss Trevelyan and her man and not labelled,' said a girl who was good at maths.

'Anyway,' resumed Queen Jessica. 'We decided that the treatment would be too complex and we didn't want that level of interference. And so we had Deerstalker put down. Like your silence with that man.'

Perhaps it was my acceptance of your situation that led you to be so gentle when we made love that evening in your flat. We were lying on our sides, you carefully working yourself inside me and keeping yourself big by quietly rocking, so that we were moving together. I almost fell asleep at one point, it was so conclusive, so safe. Not boring either. I'd had men before who treated sex like a wrestling match, liked to kick and bite and plunge, which was all very well if you were in the mood, but if you weren't (and even, in fact, if you were) these occasions were more about the act than about the people acting, who seemed somehow left out of the fun and only re-encountered each other after it was all over.

A friend told me once that a man should stay inside a woman for half an hour for the relationship to become absolutely strong.

'I can't believe you really know me,' I said, while you rocked.

'Of course I do. I really *do*, Dorcas.'

'I didn't think it possible.'

'I know,' you said, hushing the child again rather than pursuing what the difference might be between total love and just love.

'I'm not sure about sex,' Jessica said, with the same nobility with which she had described Deerstalker's rectum. 'I mean, I don't know what I think about it.'

'It's wrong,' yelled the Christian.

'Is that all you've got to say?' Holly yelled back. 'Everything's wrong. Wrong, wrong, wrong. Well, you're *wrong*. My dad had an affair and he looked much better after.'

'Have you had sex too then, Holly?' asked the Christian.

''Course! In the back of a car.'

'Disgusting!' said the Christian.

Jessica, looking a little pale, piped up, 'Was he a married man at all?' Everyone burst out laughing. Even the Christian.

(*No control, no control.* Inspector Hampshire.)

It was my cousin's birthday party, and one of those days, unlike that crucially unhappy dinner with Joshua and Victoria, when I felt pleased with my body. It looked well in its clothes and I felt attractive in a way that often I don't. I knew too that I had that 'aura thing' which you once pointed out to me when re-reading *To The Lighthouse*. You know, the paragraph that describes Minta Doyle and how she is aware that sometimes she can have every man eating out of her hand, and on another occasion she feels she is dismal and repellent? That evening, I was Minta on a good day.

We were seated at small round tables for a very long dinner. The food was exquisite; the kind that can be managed at the same time as talking because it doesn't require persistent hacking at with knife and fork. The man next to me was a splendid creation, deeply academic but not in the mood for talking about it. He wanted, as too few men do as far as I can tell, to talk about difficult emotions. Never mind that we were strangers. Here we were on earth, in the middle of a mishmash of humanity. And we felt like playing chess with these emotions, like two gods, looking down on mortal limitations, including our own, and wondering why we both found life so peculiar. It began midway through some asparagus that was so small it could have been grown in a glass matchbox. I cannot reproduce the conversation exactly, Jamie, but it went something like this:

'Do you ever worry, for example, that you might go mad?'

'Oh yes, often. Or at least four times a year. Definitely at Christmas.'

I lit up at that.

'And yet you can't get yourself involved in leisure activities that might balance you? Like gardening.'

'Yes, I must say gardening does seem banal. Scrabbling around the surface of a planet that's not going to change much for the efforts of one spade, though I'm sure digging your hands into a pot of muck is very good.'

'Yes, very good.'

'But banal.'

'What about wanting to be a woman? Do you ever feel like that?' I risked.

'On and off. I like women's clothes. I get bored of the corporate look.'

'Is that why you're wearing the cravat?'

'Subconsciously perhaps. What do you think of it?'

'It's OK. And what's your view on teeth?' I asked.

He gave a grin. 'Oh, a great worry. I like them to be white. Coffee and red wine,' he lifted his glass and took a swig, 'ruin them, and I'm addicted to both.'

'Have you tried scrubbing them with baking soda?'

'Don't think I'd like that much. Does it really work?'

'Yes. But what about sheer terror? Do you ever get the feeling that your nerve endings are on fire with terror?'

'Not quite that, but I've had the business where you can't swallow when you are in the middle of speaking.'

I had a slight sense at this point that he was talking now about me rather than himself. His neck was too fat for panic attacks.

'What do you do about it then?'

'I think perhaps I'd better not go into it,' he said with another grin.

'And what about dancing? How do *you* feel about

that?' he asked finally, pushing away a half-finished slice of gateau and looking towards the band at the other side of the room.

'I loathe it.'

'Oh surely not. It's a chance to relax.'

Here we definitely disagreed but, liking him so much, with banging heart I allowed him to hoik me up from the table. I liked ballet as a child, because you were told what to do and because I loved tutus, buns, the clean feel of a bare forehead, winning certificates, curtseying – though I was known for habitually finishing my routine at least one minute before the music ended. I thought Scottish dancing and tap (particularly the latter) the ultimate in vulgarity and as for dancing per se with no choreography, that I found utterly baffling, even frightening, and have ever since.

'Let go,' he said. 'Just shuffle about. I'll hold you.'

'Let go!' I stared at him.

'Why not?'

Having spent the evening in the arena of metaphors, I was muddled about what he meant exactly until he took me by the hand and gently guided me into the necessary gyrations without a trace of a smirk on his face.

'There, how was that?'

'I quite liked it,' I said.

The fact that he actually heard my answer conjured a memory from adolescence of trying to make conversation while on dancefloors, drowned out by music.

'Another then? You'll like this music.'

I didn't need to say anything this time for him to know that I was in agreement and off we went again, me still being led, and a few bumps against his shins with my killer black boots. His neck smelled of ironing and his shirt collar against shaved skin made me think of Stilton cheese. Then suddenly he made a funny noise. He was sweating.

'Oh, are you all right, sorry, thank you, don't worry, I can do it on my own now,' I said and pulled my hand away and then gingered my way through a tiny routine which consisted mainly of raising my arms above my head and waving them about. I don't mind arm dancing, it's feet that are a problem. (Mr Johnnie Redfield: 'That'll be your long toes, I should think. Why not try my Shandals? You can dance all night in them and wear the green suede lace-ups during the day.' 'What are they called, sorry?' 'Shandals.')

'It's OK,' he said. 'I've probably drunk a bit too much.'

Then his arm led me not to the table but to a cluster of armchairs. He patted his lap playfully. I perched in a rather schoolmarmish way on his knee and repeated my thanks for his helping me through 'something I've always found hard'.

'That's enough of hard things, don't you think? What do you find easy?'

I was floored by that. I've always been better at describing complexity than just blandly saying something like I like chocolate. So: 'I find sleeping easy.'

A lie. I love sleeping but I don't find it easy.

'Oh yes, of course, sleeping. Do you prefer it alone or in company?'

This sounds lascivious but it wasn't. We had returned to the exploratory mode.

'Well, I like both. If I'm ill I like to be alone but if not . . .'

'Same here,' he said, and scratched his ankle. 'Sorry, I must have been bitten.'

Why did the fact that this man had been bitten not put me off, as it would if Alastair or Neville or Philip Larkin bared their ankles and scratched?

'Perhaps it would be easier if you sat on my lap?' I said.

'We could try that but I'm rather heavy for you, I fear.'

I knew where we were going. We were going to bed, where we could both lie comfortably and scratch and wriggle in peace. And more to the point, in private. And because this fact had not been stated but was absolutely in the air, I felt a sudden rush of happiness. For here was an Innocent, inside a Man of Confidence. The perfect combination. We left the party together and walked arm in arm past brightly lit shops.

'Let's go for a drink.'

And so there was wine and then a walk along the Embankment, his arm once more around my waist. And there was also a confession. The first full description of what I was going through over you, Jamie. And what was so lovely about him was that he didn't wheel out the usual moral objections but just listened quietly and said, 'I think you've been very brave.'

'Really?'

'Yes, I do. You're obviously not intrinsically immoral, you're just loving. You've been, well, been very pure-hearted, I think.'

At this I was so astonished that I started crying.

It was only after we had hugged that I felt that, even in that most innocent of touches, I had betrayed you.

I remember going home to my cousin's house. She was a bit drunk herself after the party but we sat up for a while talking.

'Who was that man?' I asked.

'Oh, Tom. He's from work. Lovely, isn't he? I'm surprised you came back here at all tonight.'

I avoided responding to that.

A week later, I rang you. Do you remember? During my lunchbreak, I braved the sports field and sought the shelter of the woods just beyond it, and took out my mobile phone to tell you.

'Darling.'

'Can't hear.'

'Me, me!'

'Oh, my love, hello.'

'Jamie, I love you.'

'I love you too.'

'No, no,' I yelled, making that mobile phone mistake of thinking that shouting makes one's voice clear (indeed a mistake under most circumstances and for most

people, particularly teachers). 'No, no, I *really* love you.'
The phone let out a mighty fart and went dead.

> When I was a child I thought
> a river was a river and a mountain was a mountain.
> When I became a man I thought
> a river was not a river and a mountain was not a
>   mountain.
> Now I am old I know
> a river is a river and a mountain is a mountain.

When you sent me this poem, I found it so comforting
that I typed it up and stuck it on my classroom door. Not
a poem that children would much like, but it reminded
me of you and your educated simplicity. Now I reflect on
it, you are someone the thought of whom always brings
with it some kind of readjustment of attitude.

Perhaps it is a mistake to say 'I love you' so many
times because at moments such as that lunchbreak one,
words are not the point. One has to initiate an action: go,
visit, *touch*. And it can't wait either.

And yet one must wait. That too is part of it. I knew I
should not ring you back until after school.

That afternoon, we were dealing with poetic terms.

'He is an elephant. So. That's a metaphor, isn't it?
There's no word like *like* or *as* in it. Clear? Like an elephant – simile; just an elephant – metaphor.'

'I don't understand why *just* an elephant is a
metaphor.'

'Why not? I've just explained. It's got nothing to do with the word *just*. It's that there isn't a *like*.'

'You *just* said it was *just* an elephant.'

'Don't be awkward.'

'Or, I know,' called out someone spitefully, 'what about,' (looking at the girls who didn't understand) 'what about you are as thick as two planks?'

'Exactly. A simile. Because of the *as*.'

'Why two planks, anyway?' asked the giant. 'Why not one?'

'Look, I tell you what. Let's take a five-minute break. During that time, go and ask a friend who you think understands the difference between a metaphor and a simile. And the word *just* doesn't come into it. At the end of the five minutes make sure you understand. I'm setting homework on it.'

'Homework.' The giant mimicked, writing earnestly in her planning notebook. 'Two planks. In by Wednesday. Or *just* after.'

You were tired that evening when I made my unexpected visit to you in London, had been banking on a long read by your oblong-of-London window and an early night in the company of a volume of Shakespeare's sonnets that you kept by your bed. I was also tired. I had been banking on a run round the local playing field (safer than the woods in winter), a long bath, listening to Radio Four and an early night in the company of Mozart, who I now set to play almost nightly through my broken sleep.

I remember the train journey: again the effort to restore my teacher-tired face, and the slight worry that I would have to get home early the next morning. I remember too a strange mixture of sorrow and excitement, poignancy – yes, poignancy – as I kept myself insulated from other passengers, in the way I had learnt since knowing you. As if we had to preserve ourselves from all that was habitual in people. And at the same time, I recall the intermittent desire to know these passengers, speak to them, be a part of what seemed, from where I sat, an easier kind of life to navigate than either yours or mine. But all these thoughts were kept at surface level. Depth has always made my face look narrow and drawn, and vanity was still predominant as I struggled with the door of the train and walked down the steps to the Underground.

Our greeting was as passionate as always. Not less, not more. What I wanted to say about loving you somehow wasn't to do with our physical love. That found its own way, took us wherever we allowed it to take us. What I wanted to say was to do with our lives and our future. It would not be too grand to say that it was destiny itself that I had come to discuss with you. *Our* destiny.

I was touched by how old you looked. I loved it that your face changed as mine did. Tonight you looked deeply weary, even, I remember thinking, a little unwell. But somehow, because of your stature as a man, as a soul, and because of your height, your weight, I could never think of you for long as being anything other than strong. It was my own health I feared for.

We ate in the kitchen in the warmth that was constant wherever you went. You weren't/aren't a sun-lover, you like(d) bleak days and dreary weather, wet autumn leaves, even the slush thrown up by buses assaulting the London streets, but the warmth of inside you covet(ed) hungrily. Again, see how I am struggling with what tense to place you in.

Chips. We ate chips. Remember? Slim ones from a box you microwaved. Fresh salad, fish, fruit, white wine. Eating with you. How I miss it. There was always something of the sacred about it, precise and careful. And it was the sacred that I had come to talk about.

So why couldn't I do it? Why, after the bursting silliness of the afternoon, the jumpy alertness of my preparations to leave home, why could I not say it? It was easy to say I love you, easy to kiss you, to hold your wrist as you told me about your day and what you had been reading and thinking, but it was very hard to approach this statement about love, real love.

I have read of characters in books who maunder on about their reserve over stating feelings. I always feel impatient with them. Just say it, I think, get it out and go to bed together. Unless your creator is trying to string it out. In which case, poor old you, fated to another six pages of fidgeting with the tassel round an un-drawn curtain, or whatever . . .

Perhaps, that evening, I too was in the hands of a

creator who was stooping to involve him- or herself in these proceedings. I have rarely felt it before, but on this occasion, I did genuinely feel prevented from speaking. I couldn't even get close to what, in a book, would have taken up a single short paragraph. And nor, it seemed, could you. Ordinarily, you would have placed your two hands palms down on the table and said, 'Tell me. What is it, Dorcas? Why did you come here tonight, particularly?' And it would pour out, with laughter, tears, quietness, ineptitude, charm – take your pick, but it would be out.

Now, nothing. Displacement activities all the way. Displacement talk. Agitation. Perhaps we needed a metaphor to contain us. No. We needed something literal, something actual. A wedding or a death or a burst pipe or a burglary. Anything to yank love out of its hidey-hole and into the room as a visible, inescapable reality.

We sat on after dinner, were slow to go to the sitting room and when we did, we watched the news. Fact after fact, then comment, bloated political analysis and reporters with windswept hair standing here, there and everywhere on our mangled planet poured into the room and filled it.

'I'm tired,' I said finally. 'Can we go to bed?'

For the first time, I consciously heard myself addressing you as perhaps I always had – as a child needing permission. The habit would die hard, but I knew it had to die. I was out of that phase now and into a more adult one: I, Dorcas Trevelyan am in love with a man nineteen years my senior. I love him because I know I can I grow towards him, increase in stature in the process, cannot copy, but can slowly blossom in his company and know that the small mistakes on the way will be forgiven. I know too that this man would wait and that I would not outgrow him either – that horrible danger that trots so cruelly alongside any romantic love.

I looked at you carefully as you sat in the chair opposite me. I realised that, though you have a changeable face, your soul is unchanging as well as inscrutable. Something was going on in there, but I wasn't sure what. A reluctance? An anxiety?

'Yes, of course, my darling. Bed. How tired you must be.'

'And you too,' I said inadvertently.

Your soul bared itself a little. A snapshot of alarm and then a smile.

We both enjoy the simple as much as the complex activities of love. And one of these is the re-encountering of each other's skin. How shy I am with anyone else, Jamie! But with you, I love(d) the openness of being naked; feeling each other's weight, texture, shape again, after a week of sleeping with Mozart. I lay on top of you and kissed you. You made no great fuss, yet I could feel you rising to meet me. What was different then? What was different in the feel of your hands stroking my back, moving up and down my spine, coming to rest on my bottom? Was it that every cell of my body carried a syllable of that speech I so longed to make? Or was it that every cell of your body was also yearning to speak?

'What is it, Jamie? What do you need to say?'

I remember your body shifting under mine, as if, in order to answer, you needed to be at a slight distance from me. You rolled me gently off you.

'How do you know that I need to speak?' you asked. We were on our sides now, facing each other. My hand had moved to your face.

'I just felt it then. Well, I felt it earlier, but I *knew* it just then.' And suddenly I changed my mind about the order of our revelations. I knew mine must come first and fast.

What a mistake. What a huge mistake.

'Jamie,' I said quietly. 'The reason *I* wanted to see you tonight is that I realised, really, I mean *really* . . .'

I stopped. How could I say this in a new way? I felt myself calling upon my earlier awkwardness to help me. I didn't want to be fluent. I wanted to reach into myself to the certainty, but not to emerge it as a sparkling statement.

'You really what?'

I changed tack. 'I nearly went to bed with another man last week. I mean, I would have liked to.'

I wanted to hurt myself with my honesty.

'He was young and very clever. Witty, warm, all that. A party, in case you're wondering. My cousin's. But I didn't. We didn't even kiss.'

Your silence was as frightening as I wanted it to be,

your body withdrawing and becoming as it sometimes was in sleep, alone, forlorn and submissive to its own suffering. I told you of the guilt I had felt, described it in detail, thinking that as I went along, your body would come alive again. From the beginning, we had said we would tell the truth. Not just the answer, as Maud Scream used to point out to her little maths girls, but the working as well. 'Give the working and the struggle as well. I don't mind if it's untidy.' So I did. An intrinsically obedient individual, for all my recklessness when forcibly regimented, I recited every word of that living out of my own learning. Perhaps you were bored, but when I came to the declaration of love, deep-down absolute love, your body remained leaden.

'That's what I came to tell you, Jamie. That I love you completely.'

There was a pause. I turned your face to mine, with a force, and I realise now, a sudden release of anger. For the short time that I had spent with the man at the party, I had loved him. The evening had been a little life of its own and at the end of it, when he had asked me to come home with him, I had fought with all my might to resist. And now you were taking no notice, were unmoved by how I had struggled.

'I heard,' you said, moving my hands from your face.

'And?'

'If the possibility of this other man arose, then it can arise again,' you said.

'Jamie, that's unbelievably cruel. What I'm trying to

say is that afterwards I realised even more clearly how much I loved you. Despite your circumstances.'

'Afterwards. Only afterwards. Anyway, realisation happens in isolation. It comes to you, clean, never as a comparison. Especially in matters of love. If you have to compare a love, Dorcas, then there's something missing. The love isn't complete.'

I felt like Tess up against the intransigence of Angel Clare. I'd confessed how I had resisted making an error of judgement (or was it?). And you weren't having any of it.

'Dorcas, you are very lovely and I love you, you know that. But I've been thinking for some time about us and how dangerous it is. It's the age thing that keeps coming up. That *is* a problem. You must stop denying it. You are attractive. I'm married. It isn't fair on you. You've mentioned people you've met before and I've wondered, but I've known not to ask too much. I didn't want to appear territorial, but it's been on my mind for at least two months. I don't blame you. It's my fault. I didn't realise when we met quite how deeply I would fall in love with you. And now, I'd rather lose you than share you in any way *whatsoever.*'

'Share me? But I've just told you that I love you completely.'

'That's what you think you've told me, but what you've actually told me is that you are drawn to other people, other possibilities. And, as I say, I don't blame you. That's normal. When I was your age, I was the same. But now I'm not. You're the last stop, Dorcas.'

'Why don't you get a divorce then?' I blurted it out. And as soon as I asked the question, it was as if a very small nut or bolt or screw that held me in place dropped out and I collapsed inside. You saw that and it made you tender, because you *are* a good man, Jamie. When something is really happening, you know.

'I don't have an answer to divorce, Dorcas. I haven't been *in love* with Victoria for at least five years, but I do love her. Perhaps I'm afraid. I *am* afraid. You're too young, Dorcas. Far, far too young. I am afraid of you losing interest when I'm seventy.'

'I understand that.'

'Ergo . . .'

'Ergo, I'm prepared.'

'No one can be prepared for that.'

'OK, if you want to know,' I bulldozed, 'I have already thought about it. Let's be candid. There are men without paunches, there are men who have bigger cocks, there are men who aren't entrenched in their own views, there are men who would go on walking holidays with me, be more spontaneous, lively, less inward, less pessimistic. There are men who have more sense of fun, who are less critical, who have stronger legs, who aren't curly-haired, who are my age, who have lots of friends, who have parties, who dance – no, not that, but, oh what? Who aren't so fastidious, who don't hate animals, who are less uptight, hung up on their age for instance, a million things. The list goes on and on—'

'Exactly. That's exactly right. That's exactly why you

should go and find all those dance-loving, party-going people who also have their serious side. You should find them, Dorcas, because I can offer you only the serious side. The rest just isn't in me. And that's how it is, and it will only get worse as I get older.'

I was muddled then. I wanted to hurt you but I also wanted to hold you, tenderly, terribly tenderly.

'Dorcas. I know this sounds sudden and harsh. But nothing is sudden, as you well know. It is as simple and ghastly as that. And I don't want you to ring me. Later perhaps, but not for at least a month. Work hard, concentrate on your teaching and go out. No phone calls or emails. At least for a while. Only if it's an absolute emergency.'

My whole body had gone numb. Considering that I felt as if I had no legs, my next statement was stupid.

'I think I want to go home *now*.'

You softened. 'Absolutely not. Try and sleep. You need to sleep. You've got to get to work in the morning.'

At that, my body disappeared completely. I couldn't feel it at all. The reason I held on to you then was not actually to keep hold of you emotionally. I had zoomed right past that station into a dark tunnel. I squeezed your fingers very hard, one at a time: thick, practical, warm fingers. If I was still there at all, I had become very tiny indeed and exceedingly light, and if I'd tried to stand up I would have fallen over. So after that, I climbed on top of you, as if on to a capsized boat. There was nothing sexual about this whatsoever. Instinctively, you put your arms around me and held me to you tightly.

215

'Thanks. More,' I said. '*More*. Smack me. I'm *serious*. Smack me.'

You reached over me, crushing me with your weight, and turned out the light.

Sick Leave

The night before, walking from the Underground station up the hill to your flat, rushing with a great sense of importance, the importance of my complete love – I was going to change your life, have you take me in, become your second wife – there had been a Christmas-eve-as-a-child feeling in the air. The street lamps were gently exciting, celebratory. Perhaps that was the whole problem, looking back: I had a child's illusion that life in all its deep dug-in-ness can be uprooted at will, *my* will. The girl child's sense, too, that only *she* knows herself, no one else can see her clearly, when in fact she is to a very large extent ingenuously transparent.

What had you seen in me that I had denied? That I would get bored, that I lacked endurance, that I must have those street lights – moments of vividness, which you knew, as you grew older and favoured a more consistent light, you could provide less and less? Whatever, the walk the next morning was the bleakest I have ever taken to any station. A walk to work, emotional as well as physical work, a feeling of having been punished very harshly.

'The human body is a physical reflection of the combination of a person's passions.' Roger Bacon.

I made that up. I can't quote in the way you can. I can't even remember who Roger Bacon is. I can't do anything that you can. Envy always sets in when one has been rejected.

Come on, Dorcas, lift up your bright sword(s) or the dew will rust it/them. There's a quote for you. Othello. Who murdered his wife.

When I arrived home, it was still early and very cold. I had forgotten to reset the heating. I went to the phone, still in my coat.

'I've been vomiting,' I said to the school receptionist, who had just had thirty-six gall stones removed. 'I won't be in today. Will on Monday. Sorry.'

Oh, no problem, she rattled off, preoccupied with some address labels; of course, keep warm, what would you like them to do? Don't know. I know – difficult. Not to worry. Oh, I know, DVD. Garbled negotiations over where to find it and, reading, note-making, nothing that involved extra marking, et cetera.

Inspector Hertford: *Incompetent cover arrangements*. And he would be right. Poor children. It would be wasted time. And yet, deep down, I had come to trust the rhythm of this school, which, in truth, I so dearly loved; and to trust in how, in some way, absences have their place, are nature pushing through. Besides, even though I dislike lying, I knew that on their deathbeds, Phoebe, the giant, Jessica and all the rest of them would not have this infringement on their minds. Plus (I know you dislike this word, Jamie, but without it I would have to repeat the word besides), *plus*, I *was* sick. There was suddenness to my ejection from your life that was like vomiting.

Were you sick as well? Did you cancel your engagements that day? You had told me not to ring, that it was better not to. And I didn't. I am proud of that now.

That entire day I was absent from myself. Nothing in the house attracted me. Nothing. Except the phone. Only the steel in your voice stopped me. I felt around inside myself, a self so constantly inhabited by the people I care for, perhaps even those for whom I don't, but you weren't there. You weren't suffering inside me, trying your hardest to withstand your feelings. You had cut our connection. Gone. Had I rung you, your voice, would, I knew, have been cold. And I couldn't bear that.

Why do people act in that way, Jamie? When they say that they love? No, not why, *how*? How can they be so strong? Where do they get their strength from? Why don't they discuss things up until the slow, warm emergence of ease, why do they not care for the person through the hurt? Surely if you really love someone, it's what you do?

Or was it that you were lying? Was it that you didn't really love me at all? If that were the case, it would be easy for you to resist the telephone.

I was on the bath option by this point. Had carefully (the willpower required was considerable) skin-brushed, filled the bath, sprinkled the geranium drops, planned at least twenty minutes soaking. *At least twenty minutes in an aromatherapy bath is required for the oil to take effect.* That's a real quote.

I was out of that bath within three minutes. Geranium oil balances the emotions. 'Nonsense,' you used to say affectionately. Well, you are right. I was not balanced. I was angry, and, instead of wallowing waist-deep in geraniums, I was stumbling across the flinty landscape of rejection – my cold kitchen floor. And it was February. Unpleasant things always happen in February. February and November. I can sense you smiling. It is *not* funny.

I remember standing naked in my kitchen, staring out of the window at the garden, with its little round trampoline rusting at the legs.

Fact of life: When you've been rejected, no one much wishes to take any notice of you. Fact of jungle life, fact of biology.

Phone call one, draped in towel: X, do you feel like going to a film after school? Sort of convalescent outing? No, can't. Children.

Phone call two, still in towel: Y, do you have time for

a chat? So sorry, would love to, Dorcas. In the middle of dinner. Are you OK?

Phone call three, now in dressing gown: Sorry we can't answer your call. Please leave a message and we'll get back to you.

I could not foresee any possible positive development in my feelings over the coming week, and I worried that I wouldn't be able to work. I am unlike the senior mistress or Our Headmistress or Isobel back-to-front-legs Salter or countless other seasoned sufferers, who have developed a hard core of patience and can maintain, like a straight line that doesn't wobble, continuity in their professional performance. I wobble. And from what I have observed, most English teachers wobble, tip too easily into the personal when the semi-colon beckons: 'The semi-colon is like a split, a break-up. The two people are together, but on either side of a barrier . . .'

Puzzled looks. 'Actually, Miss Trevelyan, it says here that the semi-colon holds two equal parts of a sentence in balance.'

'Well, yes.' I had thirty-five essays on fear to mark that weekend.

I loved it when you used to help me with my marking; when we sat in your flat and took half each, compared, shared the tedium of approximations in language, sat together under the dull cloud that gathers when pages of rounded, un-paragraphed writing slip from one's lap and the effort of retrieving the order of the pages seems that little bit too much. Somehow, too, in sharing the children's writing we were adopting them for the evening, talking of them as if they were ours.

Our children.

I thought sometimes of carrying your baby. I don't think I am suited to childbirth, but I could never help feeling that any child we had would be odd. In the nicest possible way. We talked, do you remember, about the work of love being to create something beyond ourselves? The basic way of doing this is to conceive. But maybe there are other things two people can conceive between them that have as much import as the pleasure of another child being brought into the world.

A book? A new religion? One original thought?

How, having spoken of such possibilities, which are after all beyond the limits of biology, how, how, *how* could you have suddenly made the decision to oust me; no, worse, moved slowly towards the decision and only told me when it was made? Did you think it the best way? The kindest way? Or was it your only means of survival? A colleague commented to me once that everything we do, *everything*, is just a manifestation of our need to survive. At the time, I thought she was eccentric. But I see now that if we all understood this fact, we would be more forgiving.

That weekend, *still* without the green shoes, I ordered two hundred pounds' worth of clothes from a catalogue. The order included a cashmere ballet cardigan in pink. (Pink!)

When the items arrived, they were all wrong. The

222

ballet cardigan kept falling open, the wraparound bit dragged about like a tail. As for the jeans . . . Let's just say they were wrong. But I had no will to put them back in their box, take them to the post office, wait in the queue for such exigencies as the certificate of posting. I am *too young*. Just as you said, Jamie. Too young.

The Inspection

On the last Tuesday in April, we were informed that we were to be in the staff room at eight the next morning.

'I know it's hard, but this time it's a three-line whip,' said Our Headmistress, not sure whether to be severe or apologetic.

I am someone, as you know, for whom the hour and a half between seven and eight-thirty in the morning is the equivalent of three meandering hours in the evening. If I am rushed and have a disorderly start, the whole day can go wrong. As they say in Thailand, the loo is the happy room, because people emerge from it relieved. For me, it can just as easily be the unhappy room in the early hours of the day. That Wedenesday it was the happy room. All physical mechanisms worked to order, as did the hot water, the squeeze of the near-empty toothpaste tube, the inspection of skin quality, tooth colour and all the other vanities which shame me when I list them.

I had been cycling to school recently, as the direct road from home was closed and the circular journey meant traffic, but today I decided it would be wiser to drive, or my arrival, which involved much rustling around with carrier bags and trainers, would get all muddled up with the meeting. I sensed that I needed to be groomed to hear whatever it was that had to be said.

'Thank you,' Our Headmistress began. 'Thank you very much indeed for making it in a little early this morning. I know it is hard for those of you with children to get to school. So.'

Pause. She sounded cheerful. As if she was buoyed up by delight in a new piece of clothing. No death then. No accident. She was enjoying herself in the way certain people do when they hold the attention of a room.

'It is, *of course*, about the *you know what*.'

Our Headmistress had taken to calling it the you know what for some months now, first in a loud, rather hearty voice, but more recently in that hushed tone she reserved for serious misdemeanours mentioned in assembly.

Silence.

'There's been a change.'

More silence.

'Originally,' she went on, 'we were, as you know, to receive the inspectors in the last week before half-term. Originally,' (the hushed tone again) 'they were to observe lessons for three days and be with senior management for two. Originally that is how it was.' She hesitated, as if expecting an interruption.

'But now,' she went on calmly, 'but now, they have decided that they would prefer to come in for *one day* at *any time* during the next two weeks. On another day, they will come in and meet senior management.'

'But it's so near the beginning of term!' Finally an interjection.

'What about lesson plans?'

'I know, I know. But they have already inspected the documentation. All our paperwork has satisfied their questions about procedures and so on and so forth. All they feel is necessary now is to do an inspection of our day-to-day teaching.'

'Good idea.'

'*Obviously* this means,' she went on, 'that you can expect an inspector in *any*' (the emphasis was like lying under an elephant; oddly pleasant though) 'of your lessons during the week beginning nineteenth May. *Obviously*, you are no longer required to fill in lesson plans, but I would ask you *obviously* to be vigilant and clear about what you are doing. The inspectors, a reduced company I am afraid, will *obviously* meet heads of department at some point during that day for a fifteen-minute interview. But that will be the extent of it. The letter explaining their rationale is here. I know, I know. *Obviously*, there will be mixed feelings, but this is Just How It Is.'

I had been going to go to Malta in search of some sun. I had been going to go to Cornwall to read Proust (yes, Jamie, at last). I had been going to paint my attic yellow. Instead, I had spent the Easter holidays moving documents into folders, folders into work areas, minutes of meetings into chronological order. I had arranged all the texts outside my classroom into alphabetical order, had had my head in the DVD cupboard for several hours, spent a morning levering staples out of noticeboards. I'd even cleaned the windows, hoping a bit of feng shui might help my energy levels during that dreaded five days when anyone could come in, at any time, during any lesson, and annotate me.

I hate being scrutinised. I don't mind if I have requested: please help me with this, I know I am bad at this. But being watched by someone who is not intending to reveal his or her findings to anyone other than a few people too insecure to report it back to me – honestly, I find it offensive.

Why hadn't Our Headmistress told us about this change of plan at the end of term? When she had known? She *had* known, we presumed. No one had missed the date on the inspector's letter – March 22. No one had missed, either, her wonderful suntan. She had had her days in Malta, or wherever, while I/we battled with drawing pins. As a child, little boxes of pins, tape, labels hit all my erogenous zones, whereas trees left me cold. Now I am the other way round. Oh, for the trees.

I nearly rang you. It seemed an innocuous thing to do.

Nothing could be left of us when you had not contacted me for so long.

But I didn't ring. Instead, I plodded through my planning and, by the end of that first week of term, my adrenalin had slumped to the level of a Norfolk plain. I didn't care what some random inspector said. If they couldn't scrape together the manpower, if Our Headmistress couldn't be bothered to explain, I wasn't going to doll up my displays to impress anyone. I couldn't even feel a whiff of mischief in the air. The children, too, primed for months, seemed deflated by the news that they would not be properly observed. For them, being watched was a pleasant break from routine. They clearly rather liked the idea of holding their teachers' careers to ransom. They also, some of them at least, wanted to be thought pretty, clever, accomplished, charming.

'I bet it'll be some bald old fart,' said the giant during the first form-time.

'Not necessarily,' snapped Queen Jessica, the owner of Deerstalker.

'It will though,' said the giant in her Cockney man's voice.

I felt suddenly sorry for her. She had been left to grow unkempt. Everything about her needed pruning. I didn't comment, but continued, in this precious form-time, when one can simply be in children's company without having to intrude on their brains, tidying my desk drawer, scratching Blu-tack off the side of a tin and sharpening my pencils.

*

That breaktime, in my pigeonhole there was a pink form detailing the list of inspectors. And an envelope in your handwriting.

My nerves contracted, closed, left me cut off without oxygen so that I had to hold on to a filing cabinet to keep myself steady.

Not wanting to open the envelope immediately, I walked over to the staff noticeboard and read it from top to bottom, side to side, just as the inspectors would. Notes of support for girls whose grandmothers had died and anorectics off school for months, cards of thanks for flowers and leaving presents, emails from past pupils written in internet cafes in Malaysia, Thailand, Australia, tetchy reminders to do this, that and the other. There was even a notice, written by me, about a girl in my form who needed a structured work timetable. But deep down who cared? It was up to her.

Finally, I walked over to a speckled grey armchair and sat down.

List of Inspectors
Miss Margaret Maclaren – Head of Clarries Junior
    School
Mr St John Taylor – Ex-Head of Leatherhead
    School for Boys
Professor Jamie Loring – professor of English,
    Queen Mary, University of London

*

And the letter.

My darling – Life has its ways. The occasion to act
as an inspector came as an unexpected request
from the ISI. It also came, perhaps, if one may be
so arrogant, because I wanted it.
    Jamie

So you'd wangled it.

Thank god the clocks had gone forwards, backwards,
whatever they do to make it still light at five-thirty.
Thank god for some reserve of willpower. (Is willpower
built out of small resolute renunciations: not phoning,
not writing, not visiting?) From wherever it comes I
plumbed the energy to get my feet upstairs, throw off
my suit, pull on jogging bottoms, a T-shirt, trainers which
I left unlaced until I reached the postbox, where I bent
down and, in memory of Sophie, tied them in a double
knot, stood up and stared at the black slit ready for letters – two collections, one at seven, the other at five –
and knew, not thought, *knew* clearly that you were in a
dark patch.

Carrying that knowledge into the trees where forgiveness flows more easily than anywhere else I know, I
hurried down the hill, struggled up the other side, the
sun a startling ball of red. For a stretch, where the violets
would blossom in May, I experienced the madness of
panic, saw postmen morning and evening, all at the post-

box at the same time, fighting over its contents, arguing over who would take which letters, which batch belonged to whom.

It was willpower again that made me sit down at that point. I know this madness. Tiny bouts of it. A tree trunk at my back, this time an oak, I looked into you and knew again that you too were in a dark place full of unsent letters – had written as many as me. To post or not to post. Not to post. Restraint. And so, forced to it by the gymnastics of fate, you had penned an odd little note that seemed full of our joint injury.

Inanimate objects can help the solitary person. I find, at least. On the way back there was a late spring biker, but he was *under* not *on* his bike, kicking hard at the back wheel. The bike rose into the air and then stood up on its own and started running down the hill without the boy. We both stood there and watched.

'Do you want me to fetch it?' I asked, forgetting he wasn't a pupil.

'Naa,' he said. He was rubbing his knee. The bike moved with quiet dignity, like an animal standing up on its hind legs, came to a standstill in the dip of the path and then fell over.

'Poor bike,' I said.

'What?'

'Poor bike.'

'I've hurt my leg.'

'Sorry. Are you sure you don't want me to fetch the bike for you?'

'Naa. Thanks.'

I resumed my jog, feeling the return of that happiness with which I had woken in the morning. The pretty dash of the bike, the indifference of the boy to his wound meant somehow that all would be well, whatever it was that was going to happen to me.

Back home, I knew I must write. Something. An acknowledgement. Humour would be best, safest if I could manage it.

First, I had another shower. I had mud on my ankles and couldn't find the skinbrush so used the nailbrush instead, which put me out; I dislike the misuse of objects. I remembered your bathroom and how little you had in it. And wanted it.

You. What you are. A man who has sifted through the trivia, found the few things that you really care for and guarded those with your life.

I had no card in my stationery store worthy of you. Only flowers and woods and rude cartoons. So in the end, perhaps with a subtle desire to indicate indifference, I used a piece of computer paper.

Jamie!
How did it really happen? You becoming one of our inspectors. What were you thinking?
    Anyway, I received your note, your card rather. And if what it says is true, the next time I see you, you'll be in my classroom. If I pass out, put me in the recovery position. There is a first aid kit by

the computer. We're meant to provide you with a clipboard. It might be better if you brought me some cushions.

Dorcas

x

The single kiss looked silly. One kiss *is* silly. A nothing. Like a single breath. Kisses, with lovers at least, must surely come in multiples. Ah well, it was all you were getting.

It was the Monday of the possible week of your arrival, and I observed myself dressing with consternation. New underwear. 'I wish to inspect your drawers, to see if everything is in place.' Underwear aside, we had been told that this was a possibility, that not only would inspectors talk to children while we were teaching them, but they might request to look at resources.

I carefully avoided the staff room on arrival, knowing that the atmosphere would be either morgue-ish or like a nightclub again, depending on people's chosen method of release. Instead, I went straight to the form room to take the register, but was so nervous that I ticked everybody present in the column marked *Week Beginning January 7* (not an unusual slip, I admit).

'That's all wrong,' snapped one of my girl-mates jovially, and did the job herself. Ah well, one cannot change in a day.

The day passed in its usual exhausted way, everyone

wondering by breaktime why they felt as if they'd already been hard at work for five days. Staff complained they were tired, where was the sun, why was it raining so constantly, wasn't it meant to be spring. Tuesday passed in similar fashion. The giant was in a filthy mood, infecting her class with the same pugnacious behaviour – why do we have coursework anyway, what's the point, why do all the teachers give coursework at the same time, why don't they space it out, what's the point of lessons, the teachers don't enjoy them, nor do we, why don't we just go home?

'And die,' I snapped.

'Good point,' the giant said and was quiet for five minutes, then applied the why to sport, assembly, school uniform and religious education lessons. Thankfully the bell went, and I didn't have to answer.

I went home disconsolate. We all did. We all felt we had been stood up. We had geared ourselves up for a fight and our aggression had turned in on itself. But then you rang.

You rang.

'Dorcas,' you said gently. 'How are you? Really, how are you?'

'*Where* are you?' I asked warily.

'The Jarvis Hotel. Room 33.'

'What?'

'Less than a mile from you.'

I started shaking. Sweat trickled down my side. 'Well—'

'So, as you'll gather, we'll be with you tomorrow. We've a dinner tonight and then we'll be with you.'

Not *I'll* be with you, but we, a team.

'Oh. Yes. Thanks.'

'I shouldn't be telling you. But I wanted to.'

'Are you inspecting me?'

'Very closely.'

'Seriously, it will be you who comes into my lessons?'

'I'm afraid it will.'

'I don't want you in my classroom, Jamie. I meant what I said in my note. I'll faint. I will. I really will. I'll lose my voice and faint. I wouldn't ever want you to watch me teach anyway. Ever. Let alone inspect.'

'I'm so sorry. Just do what you normally do.'

'You'd hate what I normally do.'

'Probably.'

'It's not funny.'

'I'm not laughing.'

'I've missed you.'

'Yes. But you've got nothing to worry about.'

Yes. Which yes? Yes, I know, yes, I've missed you too, yes, we were wrong to part, yes what? You have nothing to worry about. About my teaching, about me, about meeting each other again. About what do I need not to worry?

You were already there when I arrived. As you were again in the afternoon, watching, getting up, quietly asking the girls what they were doing. I wished I were one of them. Detached, pleased only to be told my work was good.

'Excuse me, inspector,' I said after your second visit. 'We've been told to question the head if we feel we're being observed too often.'

'English is a core subject,' you said.

I'd hurt you, I could tell. I looked into your face and was flooded with need and also an unexpected trust. You looked older, a little crumpled about the mouth, baggy-eyed. You squeezed my hand and left the room.

That night you rang from your hotel again. 'I can't see you tonight,' you said. 'We've got an enormously long meeting. Hours. Tedious. But tomorrow.'

At that moment, I didn't feel excited or happy or aroused or anything. Not anything. Because I didn't know quite who we were any more. But my answer was yes.

The next day, there you were again. This time only once. You sat at the back in your steel specs, paper neatly stacked before you. Tired perhaps, for today you did not get up, did not ask the girls anything, but just sat. Very still. Very quiet. As if you had hidden inside yourself, were sitting not in the classroom, but in your flat, quietly reading while I did my work.

The girls too were quiet. We were doing parts of speech. *Again*. I felt ashamed that I had nothing more adventurous to offer, but I have come to think that if you don't know what a noun is and how it can some-times become a verb, you'll never understand how a piece of writing works, and so understand very little at all.

The lesson began gently. A group of twelve-year-olds.

'Take the word "fog".'

You suddenly looked up, seemed intent.

'It's a noun, isn't it?'

Chorus: 'Yes.'

'But it isn't always a noun. I mean, can it ever be anything else?'

'It can turn into sunshine, can't it,' said the fattest girl in the year group, a radiant child called Fame. Fame Wilson.

'Yes, yes,' I said, a little too severely, 'but I mean in terms of whether it's a noun or something else.'

'Oh, I see-e-e-e,' said Fame, giggling.

'Good. So can it?'

'Can it what?'

'Can fog be something other than a noun?'

'No,' said Fame's friend.

'Yes it can,' said Fame.

'Why?' I asked. 'Or rather how can the word "fog" be something other than a noun? Fame, do you want to come and write a sentence on the board where fog is not a noun?'

Up Fame got, ever willing. She had once reported that she took her mother tea in bed in the mornings and had painted her room pale blue 'to calm her down'.

FOG IS DIFFICULT TO SEE IN she wrote, then announced to the gathering with a beam on her face, 'I like writing on the board.'

You smiled.

'Well,' I said. 'Actually, Fame, fog *there* is still a noun because it's a thing.'

'Oh,' she said. 'But I got to write on the board.'

'Glad you enjoyed it.'

'Anyone else?'

'I'll try,' said a little girl called Lily Moss.

'Good.'

MY MIND IS FOGGED she wrote.

I panicked. Fogged mind: adjective. My mind is fogged: passive verb. But who fogged it? So, adjective.

'Yes, well,' I said, 'very good example, Lily. Clever you. It's an adjective.'

'I don't understand.'

'Neither do I.'

'Neither do I.'

'I don't either.'

'OK, OK, stop.' I raised my hand. 'Do you or do you not understand that a noun, example: fog, can, if used in another way, stop being a noun and become something else?'

'No.'

'Well, you see,' I said slowly, 'it's not that it's not a noun ever again, but in another sentence it becomes for a little while something else, a doing word. Like this: The fog is thick. Fog there equals noun. You fog my mind. Fog there equals verb. Foggy road. Foggy there equals adjective.'

'Oooh,' went Fame. 'I see.'

And behind her motherly warmth trailed a bunch of

others finally enlightened, as much by her sunshine as by my explanation.

'So, I tell you what I'm going to do. I'm going to give you all a copy of a passage with the word fog in it.'

'Not more fog.'

'I know. Yes, more fog. *But* it will help you to get out of *your* fog. And I want you to underline only – *only*, Fame – the word fog and use a different colour pen for nouns, adjectives, verbs.'

Little yelps followed. But I knew the felt pens would assuage them so I took no notice. I also handed you a copy of the text. You smiled again.

The room relaxed when they started working. Tongues hanging out, silence, the watery scrape of colours as they made keys at the bottom of the page, forgetting that this was not geography.

We had a new receptionist that term called Mrs Jackie Neel. She had a big bottom, put the wrong letters in the wrong pigeonholes and seemed entirely unaware of the special requirements of staff when undergoing an inspection. Other than that, she was pleasant, not yet having learnt that a touch of aggression is the only way to get staff to cooperate over matters of admin like lists of girls' names and addresses and suchlike.

Just as my girls were really settled, Mrs Neel performed her most ruthless little trick of niceness and walked all the way over to my classroom.

Knock, knock.

'Come in!' you said.

I stared at you in astonishment.

'Your phone's broken,' she said.

'I know, I've asked for a new handset several times.'

(Inspector Loring: 'Ah well, a good handset is hard to come by. Avoid e-bay is all I can advise.')

'Well, a man phoned you. He was very insistent that I should pass on the message.'

Your turn to stare at me.

'He wanted you to know that your green shoes are ready but could you send him a cheque for three hundred and sixty pounds and then he'll post them out. He also said not to worry, they're very sexy.' She stared at me now, with a mixture of Christian disgust and gossipy relish.

'Oh well, yes, thanks very much, that's very kind. I should get back to my lesson now,' I said, irritated that she was so slow to move.

The girls had now abandoned their pens and were staring at her too. She was wearing quite a get-up today: tight wool dress that hugged her pear body, tan ribbed tights and on her diminutive feet, which could, for the size of her bottom, have benefited from the services of Mr Redfield, a pair of shiny black court shoes with four-inch points.

'Thank you very much, Mrs Neel,' I said again, and she bottomed her way out.

'My mother has bunions,' said Fame. 'She has to send

off for her shoes as well but she's got some pointed ones like what Mrs Neel was wearing which work because the point is much longer than the foot. I'll show you, shall I?' And she got up again, ready to draw a diagram on the board.

'No!' I shouted. 'Thank you.' (Gently.) 'Now get on with the fog girls please, thank you.'

Ever loyal to their beloved teacher in crisis, they settled down again with their coloured pens, though the word 'sexy' was faintly audible from one corner of the room.

'Darling, *three hundred and sixty pounds* for a pair of shoes?' you whispered as I walked past to check on a girl's work.

'Unhappy,' I muttered.

After the lesson, I shook my head like a dog drying itself after a cold dip. You had spoken. But not about meeting. Only about the obscene expense of my sexy green shoes. You had, however, used my favourite endearment. So we *had* spoken. Teachers become connoisseurs of silence as well as of sound, and that small exchange had shown your understanding of what your departure had cost me. I couldn't have made all of it up. Well, I could. But not the 'darling'.

I ran after you in my mind, looked for you, and once in the staff room, I enquired where your team was convening, what time the inspection would be over, when the verdict would come.

*

'It's not like that, my love. There is no verdict,' you said that evening when we had found our way to each other and were dining in Maigret's. 'That's not how an inspection works.'

'That's how the local papers announce it,' I said. '"St Edmund's College, a school of outstanding academic achievement."'

'But,' you teased gently, 'you had all that paraphernalia on your wall about the media and how it isn't to be trusted and how to look for bias.'

'Did you notice that?'

'Of course,' you said, with that whistling position of your mouth. 'I noticed everything. The bookcases and how the books were organised, your little noticeboard behind your desk reminding you of things to do, the eccentric position of your filing cabinets, the girls' expressions, everything. In any case, a verdict is never a simple thing. There are good aspects, and areas where improvement is suggested.'

'And me?'

'You?'

'My . . .' I hesitated. 'My teaching.' I put my hands in my lap, angry that you had not offered a positive comment, that I had therefore been forced to beg for reassurance.

'We can't talk about that,' you said simply, looking at me. 'But you needn't worry, put it like that. I might, however, make a point about the inappropriateness of having a telephone in the classroom.'

'First aid emergencies?'

'Dorcas, I was joking. You did fine and the school will get its glowing report. With the exception of the receptionist – whatever was she doing barging in like that? But above all, it's wonderful to see you.'

I watched you carefully. There was a trembling quality to your voice.

'You are right, we can't talk,' I said, forgetting that you weren't in my head.

'But we are talking.'

'Are we?'

'Dorcas . . .'

'What?' I was astonished by the anger in my voice.

'Why, actually, are we here, Jamie? Why are we eating together? Because you're hungry? Because this conveniently fitted in before the last train to London?'

'Steady the buffs,' you said, quoting from *An Inspector Calls*, the play I had chosen to teach this week, not just for ironic reasons but because I knew it until it came out of my ears. You were smiling.

'And why are you looking like that? Laughing?'

'I'm not laughing. I'm loving you.'

'And?'

'And I would like, Dorcas, I'd like, if I may, to spend the night with you.'

'The night? But . . .'

'But what?'

'But: *why?*' I'd had the hint in your note sent in advance but I wanted to know exactly. And so it all came out.

The request for your presence on the inspection team had come up and you had not hesitated to say yes, because you wanted to see me again. You adored me (and had begun many letters to that effect) and missed me and wanted me, but you hadn't known what to do about it. ('It seems perfectly simple what to do about that to me.') You had wanted to phone many times, but had resisted. But you had got to thinking about all the men I might have involved myself with, and, over time, you couldn't bear it. You wanted to live with me, to begin divorce proceedings.

'I see.' I didn't at all; at the mention of living together I was as fogged as Lily Moss had been in my lesson on parts of speech. 'What about your statement that if you have to compare a love, then something isn't right, the love isn't complete?'

'I've been drawing no comparisons, Dorcas. I've talked of Victoria from the beginning but I've never compared you. You're incomparable.'

I let that go because I knew what you were trying to say and though you were coming off badly in the conversation I didn't mind. Nonetheless, as we left the restaurant, I wanted with all my will to walk to my car alone and for you to make your way to the station. It's what you deserved. But you standing there in the drizzle under your silly umbrella, drawing me into your side, undid me.

'My car's parked in the multi-storey.'

'Right.'

I crunched the gears again.

*

244

You took your clothes off fast, clearly at ease in the bedroom which I had over the months studiously made only my own again. The sight of your small cock hanging there made me feel uncomfortable. It looked so frail. I suddenly wished, ruthless or not ruthless, that I hadn't been to bed with Lawrence. His body had left its impression. Maybe we cannot help making comparisons after all.

'Come here,' you said. 'Please. Fast.'

Still dressed, I started messing about with the clothes on my chair.

'Don't you want to hear about my experience of a wider variety of the male species?'

'No. No, I don't. I'd rather hear about your financial affairs. What about those green—'

'Don't!' I said, almost falling for that blend of imperiousness and concern I had always found so attractive in you. In the brief, harassed hours between the end of school and meeting you for dinner, I had written the cheque for the shoes. Perhaps, I had rationalised, Mr Redfield was right when he said in his bumf that they would protect me from 'the vulnerability that leads to a fall'.

'Dorcas, I'm sorry. I'm sorry you've had a bad time.'

It was a feeble response and I hated your speaking to me with such desperation. You were the Professor. Even if I did finally want us to be equal, I didn't want to see you weak or in need, which is what I heard beneath your apology. It wasn't the problem of boredom this time but, worse, repulsion. That's the truth of the matter. But I knew, with all the love in my heart, that I must not let you see it.

Oh, what a muddle. For when you started stroking me, the relief returned, the feeling of home that your body has always given me. I was terrified, then. How could I, a person who feels either one thing or another, be attacked by absolute love and disgust at the same time?

I over-compensated, sucked you for too long, kissed you all over and hated myself because you loved me the more. 'Oh Dorcas, Dorcas,' you kept saying. It was as if, finally, after all this time, you were giving yourself to me completely.

And I didn't want you.

So what did I want? It was suddenly clear, as things can be when one is profoundly tired. I wanted the Jamie who belonged to Victoria. I wanted the Jamie whom I didn't have to hold completely but only in part. In your entirety you were too much for me. It had nothing to do with your age. That was just an excuse.

I started to sob.

'My love, what is it?' you asked, with a look so pure, so totally given over to me that I could only cry more.

'I don't know. I feel strange. I can't explain.' It was a lie. Had I the strength, I could have explained quite well. But I still wanted you to love me. So I sat up and looked into your eyes with a feigned innocence that hurt me absolutely.

'Jamie, I love you with all my heart. But . . . but you

were right about the age difference. You were also right about Victoria. You shouldn't leave her.'

'Why ever not?'

I faltered. You were right: why ever not? It wasn't as if she couldn't easily find another man; she probably had already. But I pressed on.

'I just think it would be wrong.'

'You've met someone else.'

'No!' I wailed.

At that moment I thought: I'll never meet anyone else. If not you, nobody. I've loved you more than I can imagine loving anyone. But perhaps I don't have it in me to love completely. I can't manage it.

'Then what?'

'You mustn't leave Victoria.'

'Don't be ridiculous. I've explained my side of things as regards Victoria. I'd leave her like that!' And you snapped your fingers in a teacherly way.

'A bit late to tell me that.'

'I know that, my darling, and I said before, I am sincerely sorry. I've behaved appallingly.'

'No, you haven't.'

'I have. Allow me to take that, at least.'

'All right. You have. No! You haven't.' I was getting in another tangle now, afflicted by my inability to blame anyone when in their presence.

'Make your mind up,' you said, with a little laugh that took us into the fresh air for a moment.

'So.'

'So. What are you really saying?'

'I am saying . . .'

'You are saying?'

'Saying that . . .' I snuffled and wiped the back of my hand across my running nose.

'You are saying that you don't love me as I love you. Come on, Dorcas. Have courage.'

'I love you *absolutely*.'

Your look of relief undid me completely. I became entirely passive as you pulled me towards you and thrust yourself inside me.

'Don't. I can't.' My howl was violent. It said what I couldn't say.

'Darling, am I hurting you?'

'Yes.'

'Let's have a pause.'

You thought it was my body that hurt or perhaps you didn't, perhaps you knew. Whichever, we lay together stroking each other like two people having a rest from a boxing match. Neither of us liked sport. Life was a hard enough game.

With an irony that stabs as I think of it now, it was your love that helped me to tell you the truth.

'I just don't . . . think . . .'

'Think what?' So gentle.

'Jamie, you're too . . . I don't know . . . too exacting.'

'If you'd seen me over the last few months, you wouldn't say that.'

I could sense awful sorrow behind those words. But

the old being inside me who saw through every aspect of my self-deception, and perhaps yours too, drove on at the matter. This time not bumbling about, lost on the road, but going full pelt towards a wall. If I didn't crash the car fast, I'd never do it. And it needed to be crashed, the whole thing written off. In one jagged mess.

'I can never live with you ever in the same house for more than two days, I know that absolutely.'

And that was it. You lay flat on your back. Went as cold as if I'd killed you.

The next morning, it was still raining. With the terrible harshness of someone who feels they are painfully alive, you refused my offer of coffee, put on your mac, your sophisticated London-man mac. But your face had an untidy, clumsy look. Ugly. You said nothing. The crash had happened. We couldn't take it back. It was the end. So you just got out of the wreck and walked across the sitting room to the door. It is only a small room, you only took about ten steps. And with each one, I hurt more than I have ever hurt in my life. I wanted to pull at you, drag you back because all the love I had ever felt for you was returning. But deep down and with a brutal stab of clarity, I knew if we went upstairs again, I'd feel the same as I had the night before.

I had been unexpectedly trapped in my own nature, which is: I want love to be absolute but if it is I can't live with it. That's it. I can't live with it. Can't be at peace. I need a kind of boredom about me if I'm to be myself.

From childhood I have learnt secrecy and I'll take it to the grave. No one will break it. And that is why all that I have written here, Jamie, you will never see. I have written it only for myself. And my Self is a lonely place.